Do not fear, for I am with you; do not be dismayed, for I am your God. I will strengthen you and help you; I will uphold you with my righteous right hand.

—*Isaiah* 41:10

For the Ladies' Aid Society and my July brainstorming buddies. Thanks for making me laugh until my sides hurt, supporting me in all matters personal and professional and for praying.

"Listen, Lucy, I know you have the right to make your own choices, but I got the creepy vibe from your date when we were in the restaurant the other day."

Lucy opened her mouth to protest, but Eli held up a hand. "I know you don't like people interfering. But I grew up with two sisters and I had, like, a ninety percent success rate with predicting when a guy was bad news." Her expression hardened, and he knew he was fighting a losing battle. "Please, Lucy, I am just asking you to trust me. I can't explain why, but please just trust me."

She studied him for a moment. "You barely know me. I don't understand why you would even care."

"It's in my cop DNA. Though, my partner says I have an overdeveloped need to protect people."

"Your partner might be right." The resolve he saw in her eyes was unwavering.

He let go of her arm. "I had a good time this afternoon helping you. I'd do it again in a heartbeat." It was the truest thing he could say to her.

SHARON DUNN

has always loved writing but didn't decide to write for publication until she was expecting her first baby. Pregnancy makes you do crazy things. Three kids, many articles and two mystery series later, she still hasn't found her sanity. Her books have won awards including a Book of the Year award from American Christian Fiction Writers, and she was a finalist for an *RT Book Reviews'* Inspirational Book of the Year award.

Sharon has performed in theater and church productions, gotten degrees in film production and history and worked for many years as a college tutor and instructor. Despite the fact that her résumé looks like she couldn't decide what she wanted to be when she grew up, all the education and experience has played a part in helping her write good stories.

When she isn't writing or taking her kids to activities, she reads, plays board games and contemplates organizing her closet. In addition to her three kids, Sharon lives with her husband of twenty-two years, three cats and lots of dust bunnies. You can reach Sharon through her Web site at www.sharondunnbooks.com.

SHARON DUNN

DEAD RINGER

Steeple
Hill®

Published by Steeple Hill Books™

STEEPLE HILL BOOKS

Steeple
Hill®

Recycling programs
for this product may
not exist in your area.

ISBN-13: 978-0-373-67416-9

DEAD RINGER

www.SteepleHill.com

Printed in U.S.A.

ONE

Someone was in the house.

Lucy Kimbol pushed her chair back from her worktable. The noise had come from downstairs.

Tuning in the sounds around her, she held her breath. Outside, the rain tapped the roof in a muffled whisper. The view through the window was black. A fan whirred about four feet from her. She leaned forward in her chair. Downstairs, it was silent.

Yet her skin tingled. Her stomach clenched. The same physical responses she had when she was camping and a wild animal was close. Even if she couldn't see or hear the animal, she could sense it. And now she sensed…something in her house. She released a slow stream of air and remained as still as possible.

A sudden thud from downstairs caused her to jump up from her chair and dart to the edge of her loft. She gripped the wooden railing, scanning the living room and kitchen below. No sign of movement. She had definitely heard something this time, though. Her heart rate accelerated as adrenaline shot through her muscles.

Her house was not that big; most of it was visible from the loft. That meant something or someone had to be downstairs in her bedroom.

Lucy tiptoed down the spiral staircase and crept toward the bedroom door. Another sound, like the brush of a broom or gust of wind came from within the bedroom. She froze. Her hands curled into fists. She locked her knees.

Maybe she should just call the police. No, the last thing she wanted to do was talk to anyone on the Mountain Springs police force. Past experience told her that the police did more harm than good. She could handle this herself.

She took a step forward; her bare feet brushed across polished wood. Her hand grazed the bedroom door. No light penetrated the slit between door and frame.

This could be nothing. A raccoon had probably snuck in through the open window again.

After a deep breath, she pushed hard on the door, burst into the room and flipped on the light in one smooth movement. Something was crawling out of the window, but it wasn't a wild animal.

"Hey, what are you doing?" Her words came out in a staccato burst, like gunfire.

The man in a hoodie slipped through the window and disappeared. Lucy raced to the window. Sheets of rain made the glowing circle of a flashlight murky as it bobbed across the field. He was headed toward the forest and beyond that the road. A quick survey of the room revealed open drawers and boxes pulled out of the closet. Lucy put a palm on her hammering heart. The man had been holding something as he'd escaped. She'd been robbed!

Outrage fueled by adrenaline caused her to dash out of the bedroom and into the kitchen. She yanked open the back door, covering the length of the porch in two huge steps. Focused on the light, her bare feet pounded across hard dirt and rocks. Rain soaked through her shirt and yoga pants before the pain in her feet registered.

She stopped, gasping for air. What had she been thinking? Even if she caught the thief, she couldn't subdue him. Anger over the theft had pushed her off the porch, but rationality made her quit the pursuit.

Along the edge of the forest, the bobbing light became a distant pinhole before winking out altogether.

Lucy bent over, resting her palms on her knees. Rain slashed against her skin and dripped from her long hair.

Now she was going to have to call the police whether she liked it or not. Her hand was shaking when she picked up the phone. Would this time be different from every other time she had gone to the police for help? As she changed out of her wet clothing, a sense of dread filled her. She doubted that the police would be able to find the thief, if they would even make the effort.

Detective Eli Hawkins saw only a partial view of the woman who had called in a robbery, but he liked what he saw—mainly long dark hair and a slender build. She had opened the door but left the chain lock on. Even with such a narrow view of her, heat flashed across his face. Very attractive.

"Ma'am, did you report a robbery? I'm Officer Eli Hawkins."

She lifted her chin. "I know all the cops on the force. You don't look familiar."

"I'm new." He'd only been in town for six hours. Now he wondered why all the other officers had been so eager to send him out on a call right away. None of the Mountain Springs officers had said anything directly, but the implication was that no one wanted to handle a call from Lucy Kimbol. Maybe she was one of those people who constantly called the police.

She rubbed her shirt collar. "Can I see your badge?"

Her voice had a soft melodic quality that quickened his heartbeat. He pulled his ID from his back pocket and held it up so she could look at it.

Her blue eyes narrowed. "Spokane police?"

"I'm a transfer." She didn't need to know that he was a temporary transfer for a special investigation, which had to remain under the radar. Four years ago, he had put a serial killer behind bars in Spokane. The conviction had made him the serial killer expert in the Northwest. And Mountain Springs needed that expertise.

She undid the chain lock and opened the door. "I tried to catch him myself, but he got away."

That explained her wet hair. The jeans and white shirt were dry. She must have changed after she'd called in the robbery. The lack of makeup made her pale skin seem almost translucent and her blue eyes even more noticeable. A pile of crime-scene photos flashed through his head. Lucy had the same features, dark hair and blue eyes, as the five known victims of the serial killer. Could she be a potential target for the killer? Would keeping tabs on her lead him to the murderer?

"You should leave catching thieves to the police." Part of keeping the investigation under wraps involved him playing the small-town cop. Answering this robbery call might win points with the local police department, too, and go a long way toward them learning to work as team.

"Calling the police is always a last resort for me."

He picked up on just a tinge of bitterness in her voice. Something must have transpired between Lucy and the Mountain Springs police. "Why is that?"

The question seemed to stun her. Emotion flashed across her features before she regained composure. Was it fear or pain?

"Let's just say that it has been my experience that most cops don't always do their job," Lucy said.

He had a feeling there was way more to the story, but now was not the time to dredge it up. He'd just have to tread lightly and go by the book. Whatever her beef was, maybe being professional would be enough to convince her that all cops were not the same.

"If I'd had shoes on, I might have been able to catch him." She raised a scratched, bare foot.

"Pretty impressive." That blew his first theory

of why no officer wanted to come out here. Any woman who would run after an intruder was not the type to be calling the police all the time.

"Actually, I had a moment of lucidity and realized I wouldn't know what to do once I caught the guy." She forced a laugh.

He detected the strain of fear beneath the laughter. "Why don't you tell me what happened? You think it was a man?"

"He had a man's build. I couldn't see his face." She spoke in a firm, even tone. Only the trembling of her hands as she brushed her forehead gave away that the break-in had rattled her. "I…I was upstairs tying flies." She tilted her head toward a loft. "I teach fly fishing. I'm a river guide."

Eli knew enough not to interrupt. People usually had to back up and talk about safe things before they were able to deal with the actual crime.

Her lips pressed together. She stared at the ceiling.

He glanced around the living room, which consisted of rough pine furniture and a leather couch and matching chair. "Would you like to sit down, Mrs. Kimbol?"

"Miss, it's Miss Kimbol." She looked directly at him. "And no, thank you, I can stand."

Her voice held a little jab of aggression toward him. Her demeanor communicated that she did not trust him. It wasn't personal. He'd seen it before with people who had had a bad experience with the police. Best to back the conversation up. "I hear fly fishing is big in this part of Wyoming."

"It brings in a lot of tourists." The stiffness faded from her posture. "I know I love it."

He spoke gently. "Can you tell me what was stolen?"

She stared at him for moment as though she didn't comprehend the question. "I didn't think to look." She shook her head. "My dresser drawers were all open. He went through my closet." Her speech became rapid and clipped. "He was holding something...like a bag or pillowcase." Her hand fluttered to her mouth as her eyes rimmed with tears.

That she had managed to hold it together as long as she had impressed him. She was a strong woman. The sense of violation from a robbery usually rose to the surface slowly, not like with an assault or violent crime, when the victim acted immediately. All the same, a home invasion was still enough to upset anyone.

She collapsed into a chair and let out a heavy sigh. "I guess I do need to sit." She stared at the floor, shaking her head.

He had to do something. "How about a drink of

water?" As he skirted around the back of the chair, he reached a hand out to touch her shoulder but pulled back. He desperately wanted to comfort her, but he wasn't about to feed into her ill feelings toward police. She might misinterpret his motives.

Water would have to do. Eli walked into the kitchen, found a glass and flipped on the faucet. When he glanced at her through the pass-through, she was slumped over, resting her elbows on her knees, her hair falling over her face.

Eli walked back into the living room and sat on the couch opposite her. He placed the glass of water on the coffee table between them. No need to push her. She'd start talking when she was ready.

Lucy took a sip of water and nodded a thank-you. He noticed the coffee table when she set the glass back down. Underneath the glass was a three-dimensional wooden underwater scene. Trout swam through the wooden stream complete with carved plant life.

"It's beautiful, isn't it?" She touched the Plexi-glas. "My brother made it. He used to fish quite a bit. He was going to help me with the guide business." A twinge of pain threaded through her words. She crossed her arms over her body and leaned forward. "I'm not sure what was stolen. I suppose I should check the bedroom."

A department as small as Mountain Springs probably didn't have a forensics unit. He could call in for instructions, but he suspected there was a processing kit in the car, and that he would be the one doing the processing. "I need to go over the crime scene first."

The glazing over her eyes cleared. "But it must be one o'clock in the morning."

"Your house is a duplex. Is there someone next door you could stay with?"

"It's for rent. I've been running an ad, but so far, no response." She lifted her head, regaining her composure.

On his drive here, he had noticed that the houses were pretty far apart. The subdivision was on the outskirts of town. He had seen signs that indicated directions to a lake and hiking trails. Given the state she was in, it wouldn't be good for her to be alone tonight. "Is there a friend you can call?"

"Nobody I want to wake up at one in the morning." Her gaze rested on him for a moment, long enough to make him wiggle in his chair. "I appreciate your concern about me, but I can take care of myself."

Lucy Kimbol had an independent streak a mile long. "Suit yourself. I do need to process the scene." It wouldn't take any time at all to gather evidence from the crime scene, but he could stretch it out. Even though she would never admit it, he saw that she was on edge emotionally. Since he couldn't talk her into calling a friend, he'd feel better leaving her alone once she'd stabilized. "I'll get my kit out of the car." He stood up and looked at Lucy again. A chill ran down his spine. Lucy looked so much like the other victims. He had more than one reason for stretching out his time. "If you don't mind, I'll check the perimeter of your house while I'm out there. Sometimes thieves come back or maybe he dropped something."

Illumination from the porch light spilled over Lucy's backyard as Detective Hawkins circled around her house. Lucy stood at the kitchen window, gripping the glass of water he had gotten for her. She shook her head. He wasn't going to catch anyone. He was doing this to make her feel safer. The gesture touched her.

She had breathed a sigh of relief when she'd seen this stranger at her door. It had been an answer to prayer that he was compassionate and not part of the Mountain Springs Police Department she knew. Maybe *he* would actually catch the thief.

Her emotional meltdown had surprised her. She did not think of herself as someone who needed a fainting couch. She took a sip of the water and set the glass on the counter.

Outside, Detective Hawkins stepped away from the house and out of the light, where all she could discern was his silhouette. He wasn't a muscular man—more lean and tall. Probably the kind of officer who used persuasion and intelligence instead of brawn. He ambled back into the light and she caught a flash of his brown hair and a focused look on his face, a handsome face at that.

Even though he'd said he needed to process the scene first, she wanted to know what had been taken. She shrank back from the window and headed toward the bedroom. The door creaked when she pushed it open. She scanned the room. Why was her heart racing? The thief was gone. All she had to do was figure out what had been stolen. This shouldn't be that hard.

She knew enough about police work to not touch anything. She could go through the drawers and closet later to see if anything was missing. A glance at two empty hooks on the wall caused a jab to her heart. Her favorite and most expensive fly fishing rod, broken down and stored in a case, had been taken.

Lucy suddenly felt light-headed. She planted her feet. She'd pulled people out of raging rivers and hiked out of the hills with a sprained ankle. She could handle this. Her stomach tightened. She gripped the door frame.

A stranger had been in here, rifling through her things, her private things. Then she saw the redwood bowl where she kept her jewelry. Her legs turned to cooked noodles as she made her way across the floor. A lump swelled in her throat. Her jewelry was gone.

Eli's voice came from far away. "It's me and I'm just coming into the house."

Lucy's hand hovered over the empty bowl. Her grandmother's wedding ring and pearl necklace and the earrings her brother had given her had been stolen.

"Miss Kimbol? Lucy?"

Footsteps pounded on the wood floor. Eli stood in the doorway.

The warm tenor of his voice calmed her. She exhaled. She hadn't realized she'd been holding her breath.

He turned slightly sideways, indicating the outside door. "I knocked, but I was afraid that—"

She opened her mouth to speak, preparing to be all business, to let him know what was missing. Instead she bent forward, crumpling.

He rushed toward her before her knees buckled.

His grip on her forearms was light but steadying. He must have seen something in her body language and facial expression, something she wasn't even aware of. No matter how hard she tried, she could not pull herself together by sheer force of will.

The heat of his touch on her forearm permeated her skin. She saw no judgment in his expression and his wide brown eyes communicated safety. "I'm…I'm so sorry. I'm not normally like this."

"Reaction to a home invasion takes a lot of people by surprise." Still anchoring her arm, he set a box with a handle on the floor.

She straightened her spine and squared her shoulders, but her stomach was still doing somersaults. "There was a bamboo fly fishing rod in a case and…my jewelry. The rod was worth thousands. It was custom-made. The jewelry wasn't worth much." But it had been priceless to her. The earrings had been a precious gift from her brother. She shuddered.

"You really need to let me process the scene first. I'll dust the area where you kept the jewelry and the windowsill and then take some photos." Leaning close, he whispered, "You might want to go in the next room."

"No, I…want to help." This was so ridiculous. Why did she keep losing it emotionally?

He bent over and flipped open the case. He spoke gently but as though he hadn't heard her protest. "Tomorrow you can come back in here, but make sure a friend is with you. Look and see if there is anything else missing—make me a list with a description of each item."

She appreciated the concreteness of the assignment and the wisdom behind it. "Sorry, this is my first robbery. You've probably done thousands of them."

He lifted a camera out of the case. He rose to his feet and looked her in the eyes. "You're going to be all right, Miss Kimbol."

Detective Hawkins had been right about everything so far. She needed to trust and quit fighting him in an effort to prove to herself that this robbery wasn't upsetting her. "I'll wait in the living room."

For ten minutes, Lucy sat on the couch listening to him work, determined to stay awake. He seemed to be taking a long time for what had sounded like an easy job. She rested her cheek against a pillow as her eyelids grew heavy.

She stirred slightly when a blanket was placed on her. Relishing the comfort, she pulled the blanket up over her shoulder and drifted off again.

Sometime later, the warmth of his voice surrounded her. "Miss Kimbol, you need to lock the door behind me. I'll wait outside until I hear the bolt click."

She heard his footsteps and the door swing open and then ease shut.

Still groggy, she rose to her feet, swayed slightly and trudged across the floor to flip the dead bolt. She checked the kitchen clock before falling back asleep. It was nearly 3:00 a.m.

His car started up. The rumble of the engine was loud at first but faded into the distance. Lucy pulled the blanket around her; the sense of security she'd felt while he was in the house vanished. Just as she was slipping into a deeper level of sleep, she'd wake with a start, thinking she had heard a noise. She slept fitfully until the phone rang at six.

Even though the phone was on a table by the couch, she didn't pick up until the third ring. She mumbled a hello.

Heather's chipper voice floated through the receiver. "Don't tell me you forgot."

The memory of the robbery made her shiver. "Forgot what?" She should tell Heather.

"Your second date with Greg Jackson, breakfast at Lydia's Café. You told me about it a few days ago."

Lucy winced. She had agreed to let Heather

create her profile on the online dating service, but now that actual dates were involved, she wasn't so sure it was a good idea.

Heather must have sensed Lucy's hesitation. "Everything okay?"

Why was it so hard to share with her best friend? Christians were supposed to bear each other's burdens. "It's just that—"

"Do you like Greg?"

"He's seems like a nice Christian guy, but I…" Lucy gathered the blanket around her as the memory of last night invaded her thoughts.

"You only had one date. You do this every time, Lucy. You've got to give him more of a chance."

"It's not that." She had no trouble helping other people, but it was so hard to be the one who needed support. She paced through the house. Finally, she stopped, took in a deep breath and blurted, "I was robbed last night."

"Oh, Lucy, are you okay? Were you hurt?" Heather's concern was evident even through the phone line.

"I wasn't hurt or anything." She stood in the doorway of her bedroom, looking at the dumped drawers, the empty boxes and clothes tossed from the closet. Her hand fluttered to her neck. Detective Hawkins had advised her not to do this alone.

"I'm sure Greg would understand if you need to cancel. He's probably already in town. Do you have his cell number?"

Lucy's hand gripped the frame of the door. She couldn't stay here...not alone. "Actually, I think I need to get out of this house. I'll go on the date. It'll get my mind off of things."

"Are you sure?"

"I am." Anything to get away from being reminded of the robbery. She should have taken Eli's advice and not spent the night here.

"I'll meet you right after your breakfast and then, Lucy, I'll stay with you as long as you need."

She pivoted and pressed her back against the wall, so she didn't have to look into the bedroom. "It's nice to have a friend who reads my mind."

"No, it's just that I know you. Quit trying to do everything yourself. But you've got to do something for me."

Lucy pressed the phone against her ear. "What is that?"

"I know you are not crazy about this online thing. I'm doing it because I love you and don't want you to be alone. For me, could you be a little more open-minded about Greg? You're twenty-eight—I hear a clock ticking."

Lucy's jaw tightened. Heather was well-intentioned. The little old ladies at church who kept telling her about their handsome grandsons were well-intentioned. She just couldn't picture herself in a relationship, let alone married. What man would put up with her constantly being gone on her guide trips? "I took the batteries out of that clock a long time ago."

Heather didn't laugh like Lucy had expected. Intense emotion saturated her friend's voice. "Sometimes friends see things that you can't see. I care about you, Lucy. I want good things for you."

Lucy said goodbye and got ready for her date with Greg Jackson. Because she was in a hurry, she opted to hide her hair with a baseball cap rather than take the time to fix it. The bonus of the baseball hat was that it sent Greg the message that she hadn't spent hours getting ready. For Heather, she would go on this second date, but she didn't need to knock herself out.

On the porch, Lucy pulled her house keys from her purse. She never locked her door unless she was going to be gone for days. Now she was going have to lock it all the time. Renewed fear made her hands clammy as she fumbled with the key. What if the thief came back?

TWO

Eli had caught only a few hours' sleep in his motel room when someone banged on the door. Still bleary-eyed, he pulled himself off the bed and swung the door open.

"Wake up, Susie Sunshine." Detective William Springer flashed a smile. "We got work to do."

While he leaned against the door frame of the motel, Eli shook his head, trying to clear the fog of sleep. He hadn't showered. His stomach was growling, and he couldn't stop thinking about Lucy. He hadn't met someone like her before, an intriguing mixture of strength and vulnerability. Plus, her resemblance to the other victims made him concerned for her safety. "Are you kidding me?"

"One of our suspects is in town." William rocked back and forth on his feet. He was a short man with blond hair so curly it almost looked like ringlets. "We're on surveillance in about twenty minutes."

With the exception of three undercover female

officers, William Springer was the only Spokane detective Eli had been authorized to bring with him for the investigation. Right now he wished he had left him at home. "I need shut-eye." Of course, William was exuberant; he was functioning on a full night's sleep.

William tilted the paper bag he was holding in Eli's direction. "I brought breakfast."

The sticky-sweet scent of doughnuts woke Eli up a bit. "Which suspect?"

"Greg Jackson is going through town. He has a breakfast date at a place called Lydia's Café. Just got word of it. I didn't want to miss the opportunity."

They'd narrowed the suspects down to four men who fit a profile, used the same online dating service and lived in this area where the murders had taken place. A woman who was a friend of one victim and a relative of another had brought the online dating service to police attention. Local police had submitted the specifics of the two murders to the National Center for the Analysis of Violent Crime and found three similar murders within a day's drive of one another. Eli had picked Mountain Springs as a base of operation because it was central to all the other small towns where the murders had taken place.

William shoved the doughnut bag toward him again.

Eli held up a hand of protest. This time the smell made his stomach churn. "I need protein."

"Suit yourself." William strode across the motel parking lot and yelled over his shoulder. "We're taking my bug."

After brushing his teeth and splashing water on his face, Eli left the motel room and ambled toward the car.

William leaned against the driver's side door, feet crossed at the ankles. He handed Eli a manila folder. "For your review, nothing new, other than the photos of the victims, pre-postmortem. We got them from family members."

Only William would use a term like *pre-post-mortem*. The interviews of family and friends had been done by various police departments. The surveillance Eli would oversee would happen on two levels. Several female officers with undercover experience had spent a month establishing a cover in the small towns that fell within the area the murders had taken place. The officers had signed up for the service so they could get access to the suspects. Also, watching the four men for suspicious activity and to see if they favored dark-haired women might give them the break they needed.

The groundwork had been laid. They were closing in. Though much of the investigation had been handled by other departments, the ball was now in Eli's court to gather enough evidence for an arrest and to prevent another death.

Eli slipped into the passenger side of the bug, hunching slightly in the tiny car. He rubbed his eyes with the heels of his hands. The investigation could last months. The thought of living in a motel that whole time did not appeal to him, and it didn't make him look much like a small-town cop, either.

William shifted into first and pulled out of the lot. "Restaurant is about eight blocks away." He grabbed a doughnut out of the bag and munched. "We lucked out. One of the local officers recognized Greg Jackson when he was in the convenience store, struck up a conversation and got the details about this date."

As much as Eli hated going without sleep, William's call to do impromptu surveillance had been a good one. "We'll get a read on the guy, see how he operates. Then we can set the protocol for how we keep eyes on the other three guys, given the amount of manpower we have to work with." Eli's stomach growled again. "Maybe I can get a decent breakfast at this Lydia's Café."

Ten minutes later when they entered the café, Greg Jackson and his date were already seated. With the manila folder still in hand, Eli took a table so he was within earshot of Greg. He had a clear view of Greg, but could only see the back of his date, a woman with her hair all bunched up in a baseball hat. William sat opposite Eli and pulled out a notebook. Eli pretended to read a free local newspaper he'd picked up at the door and tuned in the conversation.

Lucy stared at the plate of pancakes and sausages in front of her. She lifted her head and smiled at Greg Jackson, sitting opposite her. It was a weekday morning, so the restaurant wasn't very busy. Two old-timers sat at the counter, sipping coffee. A mom with two small children, and a man occupied with his newspaper, sitting with a short man with curly blond hair, were the only other patrons.

Greg said something about one of the accounts he handled. She didn't quite understand his job. He lived in a town some distance from Mountain Springs and traveled here often for his job. He was a sales rep for a feed company or something. His work involved driving across the state and talking to farmers and agriculture supply stores. A breakfast date was a little strange, but he was in town for some sort of work thing, so they had decided to get together.

Getting out of the house had been a good idea. If nothing else, the date took her mind off the robbery.

Greg struck her as a sweet man, a stable man, but nothing went *zing* inside when she was with him.

"I was thinking, Lucy. I'm sometimes traveling through Mountain Springs on Sunday for my Monday meetings. Would you like to go to church together?" He leaned a little closer to her. "Maybe?"

She had promised Heather she wouldn't dismiss Greg so quickly. "When is the next time you're in town?" Maybe *zing* happened later.

"I have some clients to visit here in a couple of days, but that won't be a Sunday."

Going to church together felt too serious. "I don't know…maybe."

Behind her, the waitress asked the man with the newspaper what he wanted to eat. His newspaper rustled as he set it down. Lucy perked up when the man ordered pancakes and bacon. She knew that voice, the warmth of it. She removed her hat and turned toward him.

Detective Hawkins's face blanched, but then he recovered and nodded in her direction. He held up a glass container of maple syrup. "I heard this was a good place to eat breakfast."

"Best in town."

The other man, the one with the curly blond

hair, cleared his throat. He shifted in his seat and lifted his chin toward Eli in some unspoken signal. As she turned back around, Lucy felt a tightening in her rib cage.

Greg shoved a large piece of French toast in his mouth. "Your pancakes okay?"

"They're great, thanks." Lucy took a bite. The sweetness of the huckleberry syrup did nothing to deter her suspicion. The knowing glance that had passed between Eli and the other man bothered her. She couldn't pinpoint it, but something about it felt strange, conspiratorial.

Greg chatted more about his work and the family ranch he had grown up on in Colorado. Lucy talked about helping a seventy-year-old widow learn how to fly fish. She angled in her chair so she saw Eli in her peripheral vision. Was he watching her?

Greg excused himself to pay the bill.

Lucy took a sip of her coffee. Any sense of trust she'd felt with Eli last night was gone. She set her coffee cup firmly on the table. Why had she thought Eli was different? A cop was a cop. People's concerns and their fears were just a big, funny joke to all of them.

Lucy rose to her feet and gave Eli a backward glance.

He looked up from the manila folder he'd been flipping through. His eyes searched hers. She couldn't quite read what she saw in his expression. Was it fear?

Greg slipped his arm through Lucy's and guided her toward the door.

When they were outside the restaurant, Greg spoke up. "Maybe I'll call you when I'm back in town in a couple of days. We can get together then."

"Sure," Lucy said absently. The look of fear on Eli's face was etched in her mind.

Eli watched Lucy pass by the restaurant window. He had nearly choked on his water when she had glanced at him. He scanned the pre-post-mortem photos from the file again. His heart squeezed tight.

William doodled on his notepad. "That guy Jackson, Mr. Ordinary, huh? You know what they say. Beneath that smooth surface lurks the heart of a killer."

Eli continued to examine the photographs, taking in a deep breath to quell the rising panic. "Who exactly says that, William?"

"You know, it's always the guy who is quiet and keeps to himself who is the killer." William rested his elbows on the table and narrowed his eyes at Eli. "What is it, man? You look like you just took a left hook to the jaw."

One by one, Eli passed the photos to William. Though the women had all died in different ways—poisoning, strangulation, stabbing—their appearance and membership in the online service linked them together. "Do you see it?"

"Yeah, they all are beautiful, dark-haired women." William's tone had become more insistent. "We established that."

Eli took in a breath in an effort to slow his thudding heart. "I think I know who the next victim could be."

"You mean, the woman Jackson was with... 'cause of the dark hair."

"I answered a robbery call at her house last night. I noticed the resemblance, but didn't realize how closely she matched her victims until looking at the photos." His mouth went dry. "If she is dating Jackson, she probably met him through the service." Eli hadn't failed to notice the daggers she shot toward him as she left the restaurant. Her distrust of police ran deep, and it took only the smallest irregularity to trigger it. She probably thought he was stalking her.

More than anything, when he'd seen the veil of protection fall across her eyes, he had wanted to explain why he was in the café, but he couldn't. They had put too much manpower on the case to blow it. Going public with the investigation could cause the killer to go underground, then years from now after three or four more women died, they'd have to connect the dots all over again.

Eli spread the photos across the table. He could not shake the anxiety coiling through him. He tapped his finger on one of the pictures. "Look. Same hair, same eyes. Lucy Kimbol is a dead ringer for these other victims."

The sense of justice that had led him to want to be a police officer rose up in him. They were going to get this guy. No one else was going to die on his watch. "I think we need to keep our eye on potential victims, too."

"Manpower is limited, remember." William rested his elbows on the table. "We'll be watching potential victims when they are with suspects."

Eli gathered up the photographs. "Not always. We have to rotate surveillance as it is."

William shook his head. "You have to let go of the belief that you can protect everyone all of the time. You are not supercop. None of us are."

"I just think when someone fits criteria for being a potential victim, we ought to do something about it." Who was he kidding? Lucy wouldn't accept police protection if it came tied up in a silver bow.

He'd have to find some other way to keep her safe.

THREE

Eli's heart kicked into overdrive as he brought his car to a stop outside of Lucy's duplex. He was probably the last person Lucy wanted to see right now. If the department wasn't going to spring for the manpower to keep an eye on her, he would do it on his own time. Besides, his solution solved two problems. Two days in a motel was two days too many, and she had a duplex for rent.

In her front yard, three teenagers lined up, all holding fly rods. Lucy moved from one student to the next, adjusting their grip on the rod handle or demonstrating the casting.

Her long, dark hair cascaded down to the middle of her back. The vest with all the pockets, a T-shirt and khaki pants was probably the official uniform of fly fishers everywhere. Her cheeks were sun-tinged. Even in the bulky clothes, her narrow waist and the soft curve of her hips were evident. He liked the way the students seemed responsive to her instruction, remaining quiet and focusing on her while she talked.

Part of solid police work involved not jumping to conclusions. He could be wrong about Lucy being the next victim, but he didn't want to take a chance with her life. How many dark-haired, blue-eyed women could there be in an area that probably had more cows and sheep than people?

The three teenagers held their poles midair and stared when Eli pulled into the gravel driveway.

Part of the profile of the killer was that the dark hair and blue eyes were symbolic in some way. The other aspect of his personality was that he probably traveled for his job or had enough time and money to cover the area where the killings had taken place. On the online sign-up forms, there was an option that allowed an applicant to restrict match choices to a geographic region.

Eli and the other officers had joked as they looked at the matchmaking Web site for "investigative purposes." They all agreed that a guy would have to be pretty desperate to sign up for something like that. He noticed though that the number of single guys on the force who mentioned having dates seemed to go up quite a bit after that.

William had even signed Eli up, but he'd missed the only two dates he'd agreed to because of work.

He'd been twenty-six when he had caught the Spokane killer; now at thirty, his life was his work and that was fine with him. He couldn't imagine a woman who would put up with the kind of hours he kept. He had nieces and nephews and mentored kids through the church youth group. He never sat at home, twiddling his thumbs and thinking about taking up watercolor painting.

Eli got out of his car and sauntered toward Lucy.

Her granite gaze told him all he needed to know. After a few words of instruction to the kids, she walked over to him. "The guy who called asking about the rental didn't sound like you on the phone."

"I had my partner call in and ask about it when I saw the newspaper ad." She probably would have hung up on him. "I do need a place to live."

Her chin jerked up slightly. "Wouldn't you rather get a place closer to town?"

He had counted on meeting some resistance. "It's not like there are a ton of rental choices. I like how quiet it is out here."

She studied him for a moment. Her expression softened. "That much is true." She kept her voice level, completely neutral. "It's been vacant for a couple of months, and I really do need the income."

If it was about money to her, fine. He'd stay close any way he could.

She stepped onto the wraparound porch, pulled a key from her pocket and opened the door. The house was clean and airy. Like her place, it had a loft. He would have taken it if it had been a dump.

"It's nice. I like that it's a furnished place. I didn't bring a whole lot with me from Spokane," he said. "I like being out in the country, but still minutes from town."

"I like it, too. I'm close to the river, close to my work." Lucy's voice lilted slightly when she spoke about the river.

Eli wandered through the house, opened and closed the bathroom door. He had to at least look as if he was considering. He pointed at another door.

"That leads to a half basement—sump pump and hot-water tank are down there," Lucy offered.

After a cursory glance into the bedroom, he opened the back door and stepped out on the porch.

"Be careful." Her voice grew closer. "The floor-boards on that side are old."

Eli pressed his boot against a board that bowed from his weight. Several of the planks were broken and there were some gaps where wood should have been. He lifted his head. The air smelled of pine. The breeze brushed his cheeks. A guy could get used to this. "I definitely want to take it."

Lucy came to the open door. "I'm glad to hear

that." She pointed to a hole in the porch. "My friend Nelson is coming this afternoon to help me fix this. I do upkeep as I get the funds."

"The porch is not really what you notice when you step out here." He pointed to the view of the open field and the surrounding ever-greens.

"It's the reason I stay." A faint smile graced her lips.

Ah, so the way to this woman's heart is to mention the beautiful landscape.

"I have rental forms for you to fill out. The lease is month-to-month." She stood, twisting the knob. "Does that sound good to you, Detective Hawkins?"

Obviously, her name choice indicated she wanted the relationship to be about business. It would be nice though if she would call him by his first name. "I did a little digging into your robbery."

"I did some work, too. I wrote out a description of what was taken. There wasn't anything else missing from the room besides the jewelry and the fishing rod." She stepped out on the porch and stood three feet from him. "What did you find out?"

"Couple down the road had a laptop and money taken a few weeks ago."

She crossed her arms. The breeze stirred the wispy hair around her face. She gazed at him with wide, round eyes—blue eyes, just like the other victims.

"I don't know if this is important or not, but I wasn't supposed to be home the night of the robbery. I delayed a fly fishing clinic because of the storm. It rains a lot in May."

"Who would have known you were gone?"

Lucy let out a gust of air. "Everyone."

He chuckled. "Oh, I forgot, small town."

She stepped away from him and stared out at the forest that surrounded her property. "What made you want to leave the city? I'm sure work in Spokane was more exciting."

He chose his answer with care, not wanting to reveal more than he had to. "Change of pace." He pressed on a weak floorboard with his foot. "So, the robber might have been surprised when you came down those stairs?"

"I hadn't told anyone other than the clients that I decided to cancel."

He hadn't seen any sign of forced entry. "Your doors were unlocked?"

"I never had a reason to lock them…until now. I'm looking into getting a security latch for the window, too."

Eli recalled the layout of Lucy's house. "The thief could have entered from either door?"

Lucy shaded her eyes from the sun as she stepped farther out on the porch. "He probably entered from this side, the back side. There is a road beyond that forest where he could have parked his car."

"So he entered by the door that led into the kitchen and left by the bedroom window." If he had come up on the front side, neighbors might have seen his car. There had been some premeditation to the whole thing. Somehow, it just didn't feel like some kid wandering the neighborhood looking for unlocked doors.

One of the teenage students, a girl with hunched shoulders and chubby cheeks, peeked around to the back side of the house. "Miss Kimbol, Tyler got his line snagged on a bush."

"I'll be there, Marnie." She turned toward Eli after jumping off the porch. "Rent is due on the first, and there is a three-hundred-dollar deposit."

She disappeared around the corner of the house.

Eli leaned against a porch post. That had gone better than he had hoped. She hadn't been warm, but she hadn't been hostile, either. He'd have to find a way to change that. It would be easier to protect her if she trusted him.

Solving her robbery and recovering the stolen items would go a long way toward rebuilding her confidence in the police. Finding out why her trust had been broken in the first place would help even more.

Shortly after a parent came for the last student, Lucy heard Nelson's truck pull up and she bounded out onto the porch. Even before she had made her way to the truck, Lucy heard Eli's tenor voice behind her.

"I could help out. I worked construction during college."

She whirled around to face him. Eli's hands hung at his sides. He squared his shoulders like a soldier waiting inspection.

Why was he being so nice? "I know I said I didn't like the police. Believe me, I have my reasons. Are you offering to do repairs to prove to me that cops are okay?" If that was why he wanted to help, he would want to hear the whole story and she had no desire to revisit that part of her past. "Don't feel like you have to be the police ambassador for Mountain Springs."

Eli's shoulders slumped. "I'm just trying to be a good neighbor." He offered her a megawatt smile. "I won't take no for an answer."

She tilted her head skyward. Partly to show exasperation and partly so she didn't have to look at him. There was something puppy-dog cute about him that she didn't want to give in to. "Don't you have moving in to do, Mr. Hawkins?"

He held his hands up, palms to the sky. "All done."

Eli had a certain charm, but something about him didn't ring true. What kind of a person gets moved into a place in less than an hour? He must have brought the stuff with him, which meant he had intended to move in regardless of what the rental looked like. Suspicion sparked in her heart. She took a step back.

As if he had read her mind, he said, "The move was kind of fast. I heard at the last minute that I had the job. So I just threw everything in my car and drove from Washington."

She hadn't thought her apprehension was noticeable. He sure was good at reading her signals. While Eli wasn't at the top of her list for renters, she had been grateful when he'd shown up. Since the robbery, she'd been jumpy, uncomfortable in her own home. Having a close neighbor might make her feel safer. Now she wasn't so sure if Eli was the right choice.

Nelson got out of the truck and ambled toward Eli and Lucy. Nelson was one of those men who showed up well groomed even for something like fixing a porch. He'd gelled his hair. His jeans and work shirt looked pressed. When they had known each other in high school, Lucy had joked that he was the kind of guy who dressed up to go to the Laundromat.

Eli held out a hand. "I'm Eli Hawkins. Lucy's new renter."

Nelson nodded. "Nelson Thane. I am an old friend of Lucy's."

Lucy placed a hand on Nelson's shoulder. "We lost touch when Nelson got a job out of state after high school graduation."

"I missed Mountain Springs and the people." Nelson lifted some boards out of the back of his truck. "So now I'm back, teaching English to high school students."

Eli lifted a can of stain from the back of the truck. "I'd love to give you a hand."

Lucy opened her mouth to protest, but before she could say anything, Nelson responded. "Jump in. The more hands, the faster it goes. Right, Lucy?"

Eli offered Lucy a victorious lift of his eyebrow in response to her scowl.

Talk about pushy. Lucy pressed her lips together, but resisted rolling her eyes. "You're probably right," she relented.

They moved the supplies to the back of the

house and started by tearing up floorboards. Eli worked at an impressive pace, stopping only when Lucy offered him a drink of water.

Sweat glistened on his forehead as he gulped from the glass.

"So would this repair work have anything to do with your date?" Nelson gathered the damaged wood and placed it in a pile.

Lucy put her hand on her hips. "You've been talking to Heather. She says I need to give Greg more of a chance. Fixing the porch isn't to impress him. We made plans to go into town."

Eli cleared his throat.

Nelson hammered on a warped board with a vicious intensity. He stopped to catch his breath, waving the hammer in the air. "I don't know if online is the best place to find true love anyway."

"I'm just doing this as a favor to Heather."

Eli handed the glass back to Lucy. "Is this the guy you were in the café with the other day?"

Lucy met Eli's gaze. A hint of anxiety lay beneath his question despite his attempt at casualness. "Yes, Eli, it is. He's a nice guy."

"I'm with Nelson. I don't think an online service is the best way to go. It's too easy for people, especially guys, to be deceptive."

Lucy's spine stiffened. What business was it of

his who she dated? If anyone knew about being deceptive, it was him. He was the one who had moved into his place with almost nothing and had decided to take it before he'd even seen it. What was he up to, anyway?

She tried to keep her tone friendly. "Really, guys, I appreciate the feedback. I can take care of myself." She was just doing this to prove to Heather that no matter how much of a chance she gave Greg, nothing would spark between them. If she went on one more date with Greg and there was still nothing but friendly feelings, maybe Heather would quit matchmaking altogether.

Besides, Greg was a sweet man, and she wanted to find a way to tell him she wasn't interested without hurting his feelings. As Lucy placed the claw end of her hammer under a nail and rocked it back and forth, her irritation grew. Why was everyone trying to run her love life?

She pulled out several nails and tossed them in the coffee can they were using for waste. Then she pounded on the rotted boards to break them up and loosen them.

When she looked up, breathless from the exertion, both men were staring at her. She readjusted the baseball hat she'd been using to hold her hair out of her eyes. "What?"

Eli grinned. "I would hate to be one of those boards."

When he smiled, his eyes sparkled. A laugh escaped her lips. She'd let herself get way too worked up. "Guess I was being a little mean to the wood."

Eli surveyed the area around her house. "Where are the tools to cut and place the new boards?"

Lucy sat up straight and massaged the small of her back. "Over in the shed. Why don't you guys go get them, since I've been doing all the hard work?" she joked.

Eli glanced back at Lucy as he and Nelson walked toward the shed. She had taken the baseball cap off to wipe her brow. The thought of her being alone with Greg terrified him. The more time she spent with him, the more danger she might be in. Was it worth blowing the secrecy of the investigation to tell her that Greg was a suspect? Given her distrust of cops, she probably wouldn't believe him anyway.

Nelson opened the shed door and clicked on the light. The shed had a concrete floor. A kayak and a variety of fishing poles lined one wall. Saws, drills and other assorted tools cluttered a table in a far corner.

Dust danced in the cylinders of light created by

two small windows. Eli's eyes adjusted to the dimness. He whistled. "Lucy has some pretty nice tools."

"I think she got most of these from her brother." Nelson grabbed a piece of plywood leaning against a wall.

"Her brother?"

The scraping of wood against concrete drowned out Eli's question. Nelson pointed toward a corner of the shed. "If you want to grab the sawhorses, we can set up the tables."

Eli picked up a sawhorse in each hand. "So you don't like the idea of Lucy doing this online thing?" Maybe he could get Nelson to talk Lucy out of seeing Greg.

Nelson shrugged. "Lucy does what Lucy wants to do. I don't think we have much to worry about. After a few dates, she'll just decide she wants to be friends. That's her usual pattern. It started with me in high school."

"You dated Lucy?"

"All water under the bridge. She became a Christian a little before her mom died. We didn't share the same faith. She didn't want to date anymore."

Eli detected just a hint of hurt in Nelson's comments. They stepped back out into the sunlight. Lucy had gathered the rotting wood into a pile and was in the process of backing Nelson's truck up to it.

They worked through the afternoon. Lucy loaded the old wood to be hauled away. Nelson cut and measured boards. Lucy brought the boards to Eli and helped put them in place so he could drive the nails in.

It was late in the day when they all stood back to admire their handiwork.

"You guys did a good job." As she stood between them, Lucy wrapped an arm around each man. "I'll just have to stain it tomorrow."

Eli's cell rang. William's voice came on the other end of the line. "Hawkins, I got a little info you might be interested in."

"Just a second." Eli stepped away so Lucy and Nelson wouldn't be able to hear the call. He ambled toward his side of the duplex. "Whatcha got?"

"The other day in the café, Greg Jackson mentioned the name of the small town where he grew up in Colorado. I remembered I had a P.I. buddy down there who owed me a favor. He tracked down a childhood friend of Jackson's."

Eli tensed. "Is the probing going to get back to Jackson? That could blow everything." The last thing they needed was for any of the suspects to know they were looking into their lives.

"Relax, this isn't my first day at camp. The friend hasn't had contact with Greg in years. They were in the same FFA club in high school. My detective friend didn't put up any flags. He just followed the guy into a bar and struck up a conversation with him. We are being very careful."

"Sorry, didn't mean to snap at you." If there was anyone he trusted to maintain the integrity of the investigation, it was William. Lucy's resistance to his advice about Greg had made him tense. "What did you find out?"

"Greg had a troubled childhood. Mom was repeatedly treated for 'injuries' until she finally divorced Dad. As we already knew, most of Greg's crimes fall into the under-eighteen sealed category, except for that one assault charge when he was nineteen. The high school friend said that after that, Greg supposedly found God and got his life straightened out."

Eli turned to watch as Lucy hugged Nelson goodbye. Nelson climbed into his truck. He waved at Eli and drove around to the other side of the house. "People do find healing in their faith, William."

"And sometimes that stuff lies just beneath the surface waiting to erupt."

He couldn't argue with that. Christ could transform lives, but religion could also mask unresolved issues. "Is there anything else?"

"While I was briefing all the small police departments who are going to help us, one of the highway patrol officers recognized Jackson's picture. Couple of weeks back, Jackson had a little bit of a run-in with this highway patrol officer for speeding."

"Who hasn't?"

"The officer was female, and he put his hands on her neck. A court date is pending."

A shiver ran down Eli's back. Lucy stopped picking up debris and tools long enough to shade her eyes and look in Eli's direction. He had to keep her away from Greg.

"Eli, are you still there?"

"Yeah, I'm still here."

Eli's pulse rate skyrocketed. He watched Lucy gather the lighter tools. He fought to maintain the objectivity required of his job, to keep his emotions at bay. Where Lucy's safety was concerned, that was hard to do.

William broke into his thoughts. "We are still trying to dig stuff up on the other three suspects. See you tonight for the surveillance in Three Dot."

"Keep me posted." Eli clicked off his phone and strode over to where Lucy was attempting to lift the heavy saw. "Let me help you with that."

She set the saw back down and faced him. "Long phone call."

She was close enough for him to smell the floral scent of her perfume. Even in a ratty T-shirt and jeans, she looked radiant. "Yeah."

"Not going to tell me more?" She picked up a bucket of nails.

"Just some police stuff." He bent over and lifted the saw. He carried the saw while she trailed behind with the bucket.

They entered the shed. He heaved the saw onto a counter. He had to try one more time.

"Listen, Lucy, I know you have the right to make your own choices, but I got a creepy vibe from Greg Jackson when we were in the restaurant the other day." She opened her mouth to protest, but he held up a hand. "I know you don't like people interfering. I grew up with two sisters, and I had like a ninety-percent success rate with predicting when a guy was bad news."

Her expression hardened, and he knew he was fighting a losing battle.

"We have to get the rest of these tools put away." She stalked toward the door. "By the way, if you are trying to succeed on your mission to convince me that cops are okay, this hyperprotective thing is not how to do it."

He darted toward her and grabbed her arm. "Please Lucy, I am just asking you to trust me. I can't explain why, but please just trust me."

She studied him for a moment. "You barely know me. I don't understand why you would even care."

"It's in my cop DNA. Though my partner says I have an overdeveloped need to protect people."

"Your partner might be right." The resolve he saw in her eyes was unwavering.

He let go of her arm. "I had a good time this afternoon helping you. I'd do it again in a heartbeat." It was the truest thing he could say to her.

Her stiff posture softened. "I had a good time, too." She patted him on the arm. "We make a good team." She checked her watch. "I have to get cleaned up for my date." She walked out of the shed.

As he followed her outside, panic spread through him. A lump swelled in his throat. He steadied his voice. "Sorry, I didn't mean to interfere. Your business is your business."

She lifted her chin. Her skin looked translucent in the early evening sun. "Thank you. I think we will get along fine if you keep that in mind."

He wanted to know if she was going to be alone with Jackson. Would she be in a safe place, a public place? But it was obvious that probing her about the date would be fruitless.

Eli said goodbye and went back into his house. He showered, unpacked his minimal belongings and then spent some time making a list of what he needed to get in town for his new home. He flipped open his laptop and opened the investigation folder. Some surveillance photos and reports were already coming in.

He came across a photo of a woman with dark hair leaving a movie theater with suspect number two. His stomach tightened. He couldn't leave Lucy alone with Greg. He had to do something.

He checked the schedule for where he had put his surveillance team. None were assigned to keep an eye on Jackson, and he was supposed to drive out to a small town called Three Dot, where an undercover female officer had set up a date with one of the other suspects.

Even as he dialed William's cell, he kept one ear tuned to the road, waiting to hear Greg Jackson's approaching car.

"Yup." William answered on the fourth ring. "Calling back so soon?"

Eli moved the curtain back from the window, thinking he had heard something. The only vehicles in the driveway were his own and Lucy's. "Listen, I was looking at the schedule. We don't have anyone on Jackson tonight." The silence on the other end of the line told him that William was probably clenching his jaw.

"It was your idea that with the limited manpower the rotating surveillance was what would work best."

Eli pressed the phone harder against his ear. "I just found out Jackson has a date tonight."

"It didn't come up on the phone taps or through e-mail. He must have made the date in person."

"I know we can't be everywhere at once, but—" Even as he spoke, he knew that what he was suggesting was unrealistic. "I'm just concerned about Lucy."

"Lucy isn't the only potential victim. We got a undercover female officer who has made contact with two of the other suspects."

Eli closed his eyes. William was right. From an investigative standpoint, they were more likely to get information that could lead to warrants and arrests from a trained officer probing the suspect than from watching a suspect on a date. "It's just that Lucy looks so much like the others. I'm afraid for her."

"I don't want to risk another life, either."

Eli paced through the bare kitchen of his new home, his resolve growing. "O'Bannon and Peterson here in Mountain Springs don't have lots of surveillance experience. I could use this as a training exercise."

On the other end of the line papers fluttered. William must have been looking through notes. "We do have an officer in Three Dot who's been briefed and is dying to learn. I could pull him in."

"Thanks, Springer."

"If we catch this guy, we don't have to worry about anyone dying."

"Five women have lost their lives already." Eli pressed the phone a little harder against his ear. "I just don't want anyone to die on my watch."

Eli hung up the phone and stared out the window, rubbing his chin. Now he just needed to keep Lucy safe tonight.

Lucy took out her agitation on the vegetables she was chopping for salad. Eli Hawkins was nosy. What business of his was it where she was going and who she was dating? Who appointed him the goodwill ambassador for all cops?

She placed the tomatoes she had been chopping into the plastic container she planned on taking to her picnic with Greg. Heather was right. She did turn potential suitors into friends pretty quickly. At the same time, it was wrong to lead men on. If there was no chemistry, there was no chemistry.

She opened the refrigerator and pulled out a cucumber. Her hair was still wet from her shower, and she needed to put some makeup on.

There was a park in Mountain Springs that had several gazebos where they could eat their picnic. It wouldn't be too crowded this time of night. Lucy peeled the cucumber.

Maybe it was a good thing that she rented the duplex month-to-month. If Eli continued to be such a pain, she would have to tell him to find a different place.

She smiled. It had been nice of him to help with the deck repairs, she did need the money from rent and having someone next door did make her feel safer.

She brought the knife down on the cucumber and sliced through. The blade hit the cutting board with a regular rhythm.

She had no desire to explain to Eli why there was antagonism between her and the local police. He'd probably take their side anyway. Cops always stuck together, always defended each other.

As much as she appreciated Eli's help this afternoon, the best arrangement would be for him to keep his distance. There was no law that said neighbors had to be friends; they just had to be cordial.

Lucy pulled two bottled iced teas from the refrigerator, as well as the containers that held the sandwiches she had made earlier. She placed everything in a picnic basket and then went into her bedroom to change into the sundress she had picked out.

She ran a comb through her hair and put on some liner and lipstick. She glanced at herself in the mirror. The cornflower-blue sundress made her eyes look even bluer. Maybe she should change into something dowdier. If this was the date where she told Greg she just wanted to be friends, maybe she shouldn't overdo it with dressing up. She opted to keep the dress on, but toned down her makeup.

Once back in the living room, Lucy grabbed her cell phone off the counter to check the time. Ten more minutes until Greg got here. Heather had sent her a text message: *U promised.*

Lucy shook her head. What were best friends for but to turn your plans upside down? Heather was doing this because she cared. Her perceptive friend saw something lacking in Lucy's life. She would give Greg another chance.

She dug through her living-room closet in search of something that would work for a light summer cover-up. Maybe that magic electrical attraction thing happened after you'd known each other awhile. She laughed. And maybe it was just something people read about in books.

She pulled a silk wrap off a hanger. What did she know about serious relationships anyway? She and Nelson had been pretty serious in high school, but she had only been seventeen. The only other serious relationship had been with Matthew. She'd broken off her engagement with him when her brother, Dawson, had his accident and she'd had to put her energy into caring for him. After that, she had lost all interest in dating.

Lucy flung the wrap over her shoulder and peered out the window. No sign of Greg. She hadn't thought about Matthew in years. Matthew had been a sweet, supportive man. She had taken a premarriage class at church and, along with the other students, had come up with a list of character qualities they'd wanted in a mate. Matthew had fit the criteria. In retrospect, she hadn't really loved him.

Lucy stroked the smooth silk of the wrap where it rested on her arms. Somehow she didn't think that love should be as clinical as a checklist. Sure, she'd had friends act on their emotions and end up in bad marriages, but it shouldn't be like choosing a health insurance plan, either.

She wandered over to the picnic basket. She rearranged what she had packed and decided to grab some cookies out of the cookie jar. She opened a cupboard, searching for a container for the cookies.

Maybe that was the problem with this online dating thing. You gave a list of the criteria you thought you wanted in a mate, but none of that factored in attraction. Sometimes people could be attracted to someone who didn't meet any of their criteria. Sometimes, what you thought you wanted wasn't what you needed.

Lucy pulled out a container. Really, it was possible to like someone who was so obviously wrong for you. Someone like Eli Hawkins, for instance. She shook her head as she stacked the containers on top of each other. What on earth had made her think of that?

She placed the cookies in the container and slammed on the lid.

Outside, tires crunched on gravel.

Lucy walked the few steps to look out the window. Greg had just gotten out of his car. He was holding a large bouquet of tulips. How sweet. There was something poignant about the look of hopeful expectation on his face.

Lucy drew back from the window. Heather was right. She needed to open her heart up to the possibility that there could be something between them.

FOUR

Eli pulled the curtain back to check the front yard. Greg's car sat in the driveway.

If he could find out the location of their date, O'Bannon and Peterson could get set up ahead of time. Lucy certainly wasn't going to give him that information. Greg got out of the car; Eli flung the door open and stepped down the stairs.

Greg cocked his head as though surprised to see Eli. "Who are you?"

Eli held out his hand. "I'm Eli Hawkins, Lucy's new renter."

Greg's lips flattened and wrinkles appeared in his forehead as he extended his own hand. "Lucy never said anything about a renter."

"I moved in earlier today." Eli studied the man in front of him. Had he just shaken hands with a killer?

"Oh, well, that explains it." Greg crossed his arms over his chest. His stare had an unnerving intensity to it, like he was picking Eli apart with his eyes.

Eli nodded for several seconds. The guy wasn't exactly Mr. Friendly.

Greg glanced at Lucy's door and then continued with his inch-by-inch scrutiny of Eli. "So what made you decide to rent Lucy's place?"

"Just answered an ad." Certainly, Greg didn't see him as some kind of romantic competition. Maybe he was one of those guys who was so controlling, he didn't want his date even talking to any other men. "You and Lucy are going out somewhere tonight?"

Greg's head jerked up in response to the question. "Lucy picked out the place. Some little park in town."

"Sounds like fun. Which park is that?" When Greg drew his eyebrows together as though suspicious of the question, Eli added, "I'm new in town. Just trying to get to know the area."

"I don't know the name. I'm not from here. I live in Jacob's Corner, about sixty miles from here." Greg angled his head toward the sky. "I don't know if a picnic is such a good idea. Those clouds look kind of dark and foreboding."

Lucy's door opened and she appeared, holding a picnic basket. Eli's breath caught. She looked stunning in her blue sundress. Her long hair flowed freely.

Lucy's stride slowed when she saw Eli. She sauntered over to Greg's car. "So you've met Greg?"

Eli pointed to his car. "I was headed out to do
some work-related things. Just thought I would introduce myself." Eli excused himself.

Even as he ambled toward his car, Eli's muscles
tensed. So much pointed to Greg Jackson in terms
of past behavior. His instant suspicion of Eli was just
one more personality indicator. Would he be able to
keep Lucy safe? Eli started his engine and shifted
into Reverse. Greg and Lucy were just getting into
the car as Eli pulled onto the gravel road.

When he phoned into the Mountain Springs
police station, Officer O'Bannon answered. He
had met O'Bannon only briefly. He was an older
officer who was probably a few years from retire-
ment. Since his arrival from Spokane, he had
spent most of his time briefing all the small-town
police departments and figuring out how he was
going to shift manpower around to keep eyes on
the suspects for the maximum amount of time.

After Eli explained the circumstances of the
surveillance to O'Bannon, he added, "I don't
know the name of the park."

"There are only two parks in town."
O'Bannon's husky voice hinted of a longtime
smoking habit. "Chances are they're headed to

Memorial Park. It's got gazebos and borders the river. The other one is more of a kid park with swings and stuff."

"You can check the file to see a picture of Greg Jackson. He's driving a gold Buick LeSabre, late eighties model. First two digits of the license are 67. You go ahead and get into position. Tell Peterson I will meet him at the station. Jackson might recognize my car so I need to switch."

"And who is the lady he is with? I've lived here some twenty years. I know most everyone. Is she a local gal?"

Eli hesitated. Lucy had implied that she didn't have a lot of faith in the Mountain Springs police. "Lucy Kimbol."

Eli listened to phone static while he turned onto a paved road. So the ill feelings between Lucy and the department were mutual.

Finally O'Bannon huffed an "Oh, really."

On the night of his arrival, two of the officers had pushed hard for him to handle the call from Lucy. O'Bannon had been one of them. Officer Spitz, the other older officer, had been the other. Lucy sure wasn't going to tell him the root of the animosity. "What is it with you guys and Lucy Kimbol?"

Again, O'Bannon's response was long in coming. "Let's just say Lucy Kimbol is a troublemaker and she has been since she was in high school."

As much as he wanted to get to the bottom of the bad blood between Lucy and the department, Eli didn't press the issue. He needed O'Bannon's cooperation tonight.

Eli drove into town and pulled into the police station lot. The sky had turned a dark gray when he stepped out of his car. Officer Nigel Peterson, a young officer with red hair, was waiting for him outside.

Peterson held up a gear bag. "Camera, binoculars and two-way radios."

Normally surveillance involved scouting an area ahead of time. Doing the surveillance on the fly meant there wouldn't be time to set up audio or video equipment. An open area like a park wasn't conducive to that kind of setup anyway.

Eli slipped into the car with Peterson. The drive to the park took all of five minutes. O'Bannon was waiting there for them. Judging from the jowls and paunch, O'Bannon had to at least be in his late fifties. He had a full head of black wavy hair and a muscular build. Jackson's car wasn't in the lot when they pulled in.

A quick assessment of the layout of the park

caused the tightness to return to Eli's chest. Other than a small pavilion with picnic tables and two gazebos, the ground was more forest than park. The landscape provided a thousand places where someone could disappear from view.

A quick scan of the area revealed about ten to twelve people walking dogs, sitting on benches and eating at picnic tables. A couple emerged from a clump of trees. It wasn't Jackson and Lucy. Her blue sundress would make her easy enough to keep track of.

Eli handed each of the men a radio. "This is far from the ideal, but it will be a good training exercise. Let's focus on making sure we don't lose track of the suspect and his date, and staying in communication."

"One of the rules of surveillance is that most people aren't very observant. If you don't do anything to call attention to yourself, nobody will remember you." Peterson grinned. "I remember that from the academy training. Hunting down stolen bicycles doesn't give you much of a chance to use that."

Eli patted Peterson on the shoulder. He liked his enthusiasm. "In the future, we will assign you to a different town for surveillance so there is less chance of you being recognized."

O'Bannon hung back a few feet. "So why are we doing this?"

During the briefing, even before Eli had brought up the question about Lucy's past relationship with the department, O'Bannon had not seemed excited about the added duties involved in the serial killer investigation.

Eli planted his feet. "I have concerns about Greg Jackson. Right now, he looks like our strongest suspect. I want to make sure the woman he is with stays safe tonight." He didn't use Lucy's name on purpose. "That's our job as officers—right, O'Bannon…to keep citizens safe?" Eli pulled a baseball hat out of the gear bag. "People are less likely to notice your face if you have this on."

O'Bannon drew his head back and wrinkled his nose as though he smelled something bad but took the hat Eli handed him. "I know that," O'Bannon mumbled.

"Peterson, why don't you come with me?" He handed the camera to the younger officer. "We'll be able to get a clear shot undetected if they go to that half of the park. O'Bannon, you take the bench. Alert us when they arrive. Move as needed to keep them in view."

Moments after Eli and Peterson slipped behind

the trees that provided cover, O'Bannon's voice vibrated through the radio.

"They've pulled into the lot."

Crouching in the trees, Eli put the binoculars up to his eyes. Lucy and Greg made their way across the grass to the gazebo. They stopped for a moment to talk to a young woman that Lucy seemed to know. Greg's body language, all but stepping between Lucy and the girl, suggested impatience. Finally, he tugged on Lucy's arm.

Peterson clicked off several shots on the camera.

Rain had begun to sprinkle as the couple slipped under the gazebo. Lucy pulled plastic containers out of the picnic basket. Greg paced, placed his hands on his hips, looked at the sky and then threw up his arms. Though Eli could not hear the conversation, the body language suggested that Greg was upset and Lucy was placating him.

Eli handed Peterson the binoculars and took the camera. "You don't have to hear a conversation to discern personality traits. What can you conclude about our suspect from watching him?"

Greg jabbed his finger at the downpour of rain, and Lucy wrapped a hand around his wrist and pointed back at the picnic basket. Greg pulled away and crossed his arms glaring skyward.

Peterson peered through the binoculars. "The guy doesn't seem very relaxed."

Lucy relented and gathered the items back into the basket. Even at this distance, Greg's scowl was obvious as they made their way back to the car. Were they leaving because of the rain or was there some other reason? Greg had glanced toward the trees several times, but Eli doubted they had been spotted.

Lucy smiled and laughed as she made her way across the lot. At one point, she turned her head up toward the sky, taking a moment to allow the rain to sprinkle on her face.

Eli spoke through the two-way to O'Bannon. "You can get to your car faster than we can. Tail them. Keep us advised of their 10-22."

He watched as O'Bannon lumbered to his feet. Snails moved faster. Eli signaled to Peterson that they needed to get going. He pointed through the middle of the park, indicating the direction he wanted Peterson to go.

Eli followed the tree line as long as he could before cutting toward the pavilion. Greg's Buick pulled out onto the road. No sign of O'Bannon's car yet.

The road and lot slipped out of view as he moved behind the pavilion.

Eli's heart beat a little faster. Where was Greg taking Lucy? They could have stayed dry under the gazebo. Maybe the place wasn't secluded enough for Jackson. O'Bannon was just leaving the lot when Eli came around the side of the pavilion. A little time delay with a rolling tail made sense, but O'Bannon seemed to be taking his sweet time. Peterson was already behind the wheel of his car.

Eli slipped in and peered through the windshield. O'Bannon turned left at the top of the road that led out of the park.

"Let's wait just a minute here," Eli instructed. O'Bannon's car slipped out of view. Eli clicked on the radio. "Do you have a visual on the car?"

"No," O'Bannon snapped. "I'll let you know when I do."

Eli addressed Peterson. "Our target could have gone either way. Let's take a right at the top of this road."

Their car passed a convenience store. Downtown Mountain Springs with its turn-of-the-century brick buildings came into view.

Peterson drove slowly past a drugstore and an attorney's office. "Maybe they just decided to catch a meal in town, huh?"

"Where do people take a date around here?"

Peterson snorted. "They usually take them out of town. Here, besides the fast-food places, there's Lydia's Café, and the Oasis bar serves steaks and burgers."

"Let's go there." They drove by the parking lots of both Lydia's and the Oasis. No sign of the Buick. The rising sense of panic returned. O'Bannon should have checked in by now.

Peterson pulled out of the Oasis parking lot while Eli scanned the street for Greg's car.

"What now?"

"Any other date hangouts?"

"Not sure about that. I've been married for ten years. When the weather is nice the mountains and lakes are a big draw."

That was what Eli was afraid of.

Eli's radio clicked.

"They just turned into the Hyalite Hills," O'Bannon said. "Doesn't she live up here? Looks like their date is over. You want me to keep following them?"

Eli relaxed. "Watch the road and let me know when Jackson pulls out and where he is headed."

Eli and Peterson returned to the police station so Eli could retrieve his car. After he told Peterson he had done a good job, Eli got into his car and drove to the local market to get supplies for his new place. He was in the checkout line at the grocery store when his cell phone rang.

"O'Bannon here. Jackson still hasn't pulled out. I'm off shift in thirty minutes."

Eli rolled his eyes. Heaven forbid that O'Bannon should stay longer than his shift required. He was going to have to talk to the chief about O'Bannon's attitude. "I can handle it."

Eli got in his car and drove back to the duplex. Both Lucy and Greg's cars were still here. So the date wasn't over. Tension snaked around Eli's torso.

He grabbed his groceries and walked up the stairs to the porch. While he stuck his key in the lock, he leaned back to see if he could catch any movement in Lucy's place. The curtains were drawn, allowing only a thin sliver of light to escape.

He stepped inside his own place and paced the floor. He'd rest easy if he knew she was okay. Greg wasn't likely to try anything if he knew Eli was next door. All he needed was an excuse to knock on her door.

Rain sprinkled from the sky and lightning flashed some distance away as he made his way across the wooden floorboards of the wraparound porch. He banged on the door.

He heard footsteps and then Lucy swung the door open. Behind her, he could see that a picnic had been set up on the coffee table. Greg sat cross-legged, munching on a sandwich. Soft jazzy music spilled from the CD player.

The pinched expression on Lucy's face told him she was not happy about the interruption, or maybe being with Greg was making her tense. "You're back."

"Work took less time than I thought it would."

She studied him long enough for him to become nervous. He shifted his weight from foot to foot. She'd changed out of the wet blue sundress into a silky floral dress. The heart-shaped neckline made her neck look swanlike. For a woman who spent a lot of time outdoors, her skin was like porcelain.

Greg cleared his throat and scratched the back of his head. His stiff posture and the way he kept clearing his throat indicated he resented the interruption.

Eli turned toward Lucy. "Sorry to bother you. I thought I would come over and get that written description of your stolen items."

Her lips parted slightly. "I think I left it up in the loft."

She backed away from the door, which allowed him to step inside.

"Let me go look for it." Lucy tromped up the stairs to the loft. She lifted papers and put them back on the table. Upstairs, cupboards screeched open and shut with the slapping sound of wood against wood.

Maybe he could learn something about Greg without him realizing he was being questioned. Eli rocked on his feet and shoved his hands in his pockets, gauging Greg's reaction.

Greg Jackson took a sip of iced tea. "So you like Mountain Springs so far?" Despite the friendliness of the question, his expression was harder than stone and his words could freeze water. He really didn't like having Eli around.

"You and Lucy seem pretty serious."

Greg tossed a paper napkin on the table. "Not as serious as I would like to be."

"Dating anyone else from the online service?"

Greg's chin jerked up. "Lucy told *you* we found each other on the service?"

Of course it didn't make sense to Greg that a first-day renter could know such a detail about Lucy's life, but Greg's instant suspicion seemed a little over the top.

Eli nodded. "She and Nelson were talking about it this afternoon when we were repairing the back porch."

"Oh, I see. You helped her with *that* repair." Greg set his bottle of iced tea on the table. "If you must know, I've met some real nice Christian women through the service. But they all seem kind of…desperate to be married…not an attractive quality."

Eli paced across the living room to the kitchen. "Lucy's not that way?" He did a quick survey of the food laid out on the coffee table. Probably nothing there that could be easily poisoned.

Upstairs, Lucy shuffled through her pile of papers again.

Greg shot to his feet. "Do you need some help up there, Lucy?" He cast a furtive glower toward Eli.

The longer Eli talked with Greg, the less he liked the idea of him being alone with Lucy.

Lucy leaned on the railing and peered down. "I got it under control." She disappeared from view. A moment later, she swept down the stairs. "I can't find it." It sounded as if she was demanding something, rather than making a statement.

"It would be helpful in recovering the stolen items." Eli's mind scanned through the possibilities of what he could say or do so Greg would leave. Maybe if he just stayed long enough.

She put up her hand. "It makes me crazy when I can't find something."

Now she was upset. Eli pressed his teeth together. He had firmly established himself in the role of the rude neighbor, the unintended consequence of his desire to protect Lucy. In the long run, the choice might defeat his purpose altogether. It certainly wasn't making her like or trust him any better.

She walked over to the kitchen and scanned the countertops. "I started working on it in here, then I went upstairs and then…" In a rush of energy, she opened a kitchen drawer and held up a piece of paper. "Aha."

Obviously not happy, Greg smashed a cookie into the coffee table until it was nothing but crumbs. His mouth was drawn into a tight line.

She returned to the living room and shoved the piece of paper toward him. "Told you I knew where it was."

The subtext of her words was obvious: *now you can go.*

"You were smart to have your picnic inside." Eli angled his body toward the window. "That storm is really picking up." He just couldn't leave her alone with this guy.

Lucy's glance flickered from Eli, then to Greg. She had probably picked up on the smoldering ember of antagonism between the two men. "We actually drove into town and then realized it wasn't going to work." She glanced at Greg.

Eli planted his feet. He stared at the piece of paper. She'd provided an extensive written description and drawn pictures of the jewelry pieces. "Nice drawings."

She smiled at his comment. "We can't all be van Gogh."

Eli laughed. The moment of humor sparked a connection between them.

Greg cleared his throat and spat out his words. "I should probably just be going. I still have to drive back home tonight."

"No, Greg. Please stay." Her plea sounded halfhearted.

Despite the triumph he felt at getting Greg to leave, Eli kept his tone friendly. "Sounds like a good idea. Maybe you can beat the storm before it gets too bad."

Greg grabbed his coat. "Thanks for the nice picnic." He kissed Lucy on the cheek.

She tensed when he kissed her on the cheek. Nothing in her body language suggested Lucy had anything but friendly feelings for Greg.

Both Lucy and Eli stared at the floor while Greg's footsteps tapped on the wood, the door swung open and closed. Outside, his car started up.

"Looks like you had a pretty nice picnic."

"Things worked out okay." Her voice dropped

half an octave. "Despite the interruption." She gathered plates and glasses off the coffee table.

He picked up some of the empty plastic containers and followed her into the kitchen. "He seems to like you quite a bit." If Lucy's reaction to the kiss was any indication, maybe this was going to be their last date.

Lucy yanked the plastic containers out of his hands. "Mr. Hawkins, I don't appreciate the way you are probing into my life, and I don't know why you felt the need to cut my date short."

She wasn't angry, just upset. He didn't blame her. He wondered if he wasn't driving her toward Greg with all his objections and interferences. Maybe there was a way to smooth things over. "I was thinking about your robbery. Sometimes thieves pawn things off after they steal them. Maybe tomorrow we could check some of the pawn-shops together. You know what the fishing pole and jewelry looked like."

"I really don't have time to do that. You are the policeman. You have the detailed descriptions." She slammed a cupboard door shut.

There was nothing more he could say. "I'll get that rent and deposit check to you." He turned to go.

Her words pelted against his back as he made

his way toward the door. "You can just bring it by tomorrow or, better yet, tape it to my door."

Eli trudged back to his side of the house. Rain slashed down in straight lines instead of in drops. Lightning flashed in the sky, followed almost immediately by thunder that shook the house. Eli stepped back into his side of the duplex. He had managed to keep Lucy safe for one night, but he had done nothing to win her trust. Her overt rejection of him stung in a way he hadn't expected.

Might as well concentrate on work, the part of his life that made sense. He pulled his laptop out of his briefcase and set it up on the table by the window, where he had a clear view of the storm. Eli clicked through his e-mails. Each surveillance team was required to send reports to him for review.

Officer Smith's date with one of the other suspects must have been uneventful. If anything had happened, he would have gotten a call right away. They had begun to compile photographs of the men with their dates.

What had he learned about Greg Jackson in their short interaction? Greg made a pretense of being a go-with-the-flow country boy, but he had a moodiness that he tried to cover up. An underlying irritation peeked out when plans got disrupted, and he seemed unnecessarily jealous. Not exactly what you would call hard evidence, but it did match the part of the profile that suggested their killer was controlling.

He had a gut feeling about Greg Jackson, but arrests couldn't be made based on feelings. As far as he knew, Lucy had not connected with any of the other suspects on the online service. Yet, given her appearance, she was a likely next target.

All the other victims had lived alone and been only loosely attached to family members. The victims had not been talkative about their romantic lives. When friends and family members were interviewed, they could only offer vague personality and character descriptions of the men the victims had been dating. Based on that, the killer probably dated his victims only a few times. Long enough to start to learn someone's habits, but not long enough to be introduced to friends and family members. None of the victims' computers revealed any e-mail exchanges that could have pointed to a killer. This guy was careful.

Lucy had friends, Nelson and Heather, but the only family member she had mentioned was a brother. She talked about him in such cryptic terms that Eli wondered if they had had a falling out or if something had happened to the brother.

He flipped through files, rereading the interviews done with people who had known the victims. He made a call to a local officer in a town called Cragmore where they would be doing surveillance tomorrow night. Eli sat back in his chair.

He stared at the rain falling outside. It was coming down so heavily that he could barely make out the trees that surrounded Lucy's place. He pulled a piece of paper out of his briefcase and wrote out the names of each of the four suspects. In list form, he scribbled everything he knew about each suspect. All of the men were in a profession that allowed for a level of travel. Both Greg Jackson and another suspect, Neil Fender, had minor police records.

Wind rattled the windows, and the thunder sounded like it was on top of the house. Eli browned some hamburger he had picked up in town and tossed in tomatoes and cheese. He ate directly out of the pan while he stood at the window, thinking.

He made a decision to keep up the surveillance for a few more weeks and then reassess their whole approach. If they didn't see a pattern of someone who was consistently picking dark-haired, blue-eyed women, it would be a waste of manpower and resources to continue. What he liked about the setup was that it allowed him to keep the potential victims safe.

The truth was they could plan until they were blue in the face. What usually broke any investigation was sheer luck. Sometimes, a suspect did something revealing while under surveillance, or a neighbor noticed suspicious activity. Even though investigative diligence had to happen, it was almost always the piece of information that they accidentally stumbled on in the course of investigation that brought things together.

Eli sauntered back into the kitchen and placed the empty pan in the sink. He grinned. He had no dishwashing soap. What would Lucy say if he knocked on her door again? He settled into the chair in the living room. Wind shook the window and the rain pattered so intensely on the roof it sounded like pebbles bouncing around in a can.

A thudding noise caused him to jump. Lucy burst out of her side of the duplex. Through the distortion created by the storm, he could barely make out that she was pulling on a rain jacket as she raced to her van. What on earth was she doing going out in this kind of storm?

FIVE

Adrenaline surged through Lucy as she raced out of her house and jumped off the porch. The sky was already dark. The wind blew so hard, the rain came at her sideways.

When she got to her car, she fumbled in her pocket for the key.

Maybe she should get someone to help her. The call about her boat from her down-river neighbor had come in less than five minutes ago. That was five minutes of valuable time she'd already lost. She touched her cell phone in the pocket of her raincoat. She'd have to call as she was driving. Who would come out in this kind of storm anyway? Who was close enough?

Eli was right next door. She brushed the idea away. They were not off to a very good start at being neighborly. He had tried her patience, and she had been abrupt with him. The look of hurt on his face when she'd said she wasn't interested in going to the pawnshops had put a barb in her heart, but she didn't want to do anything to make him think it was okay to interfere in her life. Best keep her distance where Eli Hawkins was concerned.

I know I have a hard time asking for help, but please, Lord, send someone to give me a hand with this.

Lucy dropped her keys as she pulled them out of her pocket. With the rain pelting her coat, she groped on the muddy ground for a moment before she found them. She climbed into the cab of her van, wiping her muddy hands on her jeans.

She jammed the key in the ignition. A tap at her window caused her to turn suddenly. She rolled down the window.

Eli, rain beating hard against his face, stood there. "Where are you headed?"

"One of my drift boats broke free. I have to get it back." The kids she'd taught today must have been careless when they'd tied it to the dock.

"In this weather? That sounds dangerous."

She wasn't about to let him talk her out of this. "That boat is my livelihood." She leaned toward the steering wheel, turning the key in the ignition. She spoke above the sound of the engine. "I can't wait until the sun is shining and risk it being battered to pieces or lost."

He crossed his arms over his chest, obviously chilled from the cold. "You'll need help."

That much was true. "I got it under control." The last person she needed help from was a date destroyer like Eli Hawkins. She would rather do this herself.

Eli blinked the rain out of his eyes. "Okay."

He disappeared. Lucy shifted into Reverse. The passenger-side door opened, and he slid in. He combed his rain-slicked hair back from his forehead. "Let's go."

How nervy. She backed the van up and turned it around. "Get out of my car."

"Could you be honest with yourself for one moment?" He leaned toward her. "You can't do this alone. Every second we spend debating might cost you your boat."

She gritted her teeth and pressed the accelerator. He was right, of course. "The neighbors said they saw it lodged in a bunch of branches that have built up on a slow part of the river." She turned onto a dirt road that led into thick forest. "If it breaks free, it's going to be almost impossible to recover." They both bounced in their seats as she accelerated over the bumpy road.

Eli gripped the dashboard. "How are you going

to know where to find the boat?" His voice vibrated from the jarring motion of the car.

"The pile of branches they are talking about is in an eddy just before Spanish Point." Talking about this made her even more anxious.

"Impressive, you know every bend and branch in the river."

She'd grown up on the river. Eddies, rapids and bends were like street signs to her. "River gets real rough after that. In this storm, it will be even rougher." Her voice wavered. Her business was a bootstrap operation as it was. She couldn't lose that boat.

Lucy steered the van out of the trees, and the river below came into view.

Eli craned his neck to look in the back of the vehicle, where she stored her equipment for guiding and teaching. "Are we going to need any of that stuff?"

Lucy glanced at Eli. He raised an eyebrow. Now she was impressed. "Way to think ahead." She turned her attention to the rough road in front of her. The vehicle shifted side to side in the mud. "Grab two pairs of waders. The river is going to be cold."

He unclicked his seat belt and crawled into the back. "You have everything but the kitchen sink in here."

When she looked over her shoulder, he was holding up her supply of dehydrated food. The jerking motion of the car on the rough road caused him to sway. "I'm responsible for people who may not have a lot of wilderness experience. I have to plan for every contingency."

She turned off the road. The van lumbered down the hill toward the river. She'd be able to get her vehicle within a hundred yards of the river. She bounced in her seat.

Eli let out a *whoa!*

In the rearview mirror, she watched Eli rubbing his head. She cringed. "Sorry, I can't make it any smoother."

"No problem." He flopped a life jacket over the passenger-side seat. "Will we need this?"

He sure wanted to bring a lot to rescue a boat. "Take it if you want. The river's not that deep. Those things slow you down. The big issue is the cold. Get the waders."

Lucy edged the van as close to the river as she dared, not wanting to risk getting stuck. She braked, pushed the door open and raced to the back of her vehicle. She flung the door open. Eli handed her the waders and jumped out.

The river roared in her ears. Rain poured from the sky.

"Got these for us, too." He held up two flashlights.

"Good thinking." His efficiency was admirable. She took a flashlight, flipped open a storage box in the van and pulled out a rain poncho. He was probably already chilled from the rain, but there was no time to retrieve dry clothes for him. "Put this on. It's easy to slip off when you put on your waders."

Rivulets of rain trickled down his face. "Should have remembered a coat on my way out of the house."

She patted his shoulder before grabbing a coil of rope off a hook in the car. She scrambled down the hill yelling over her shoulder. "It's slick. Walk sideways. We'll put the waders on at the bottom of the hill."

Halfway to the bank, she swept her light across the river. At this time of year, it stayed light late into the evening, but a covering of gray clouds dimmed her view. The flashlight had been a good idea. The boat was still in the pile of sticks across the river. Hard waves threatened to break it loose.

Eli came up beside her. Without a word, he slipped the rope off her shoulder.

She didn't realize how much the weight had been slowing her until he took it. "Thanks."

Raindrops, made sharp by the intense wind, jabbed at her face and hands. Lucy and Eli came to the riverbank. She kicked off her shoes and eased into her waders. Her raincoat had kept her top half pretty dry, but her jeans were already soaked, which made the process of getting in the waders even more arduous. She clicked the straps over her shoulders. Eli struggled with the drawstring around the waist of his waders. "Here." She pulled him toward her by his shoulder straps and tightened his drawstring. He stood five inches taller than she. His breath caressed her cheek. She tilted her head, and when she looked into his eyes, she completely forgot what she had intended to say.

Eli grinned, his face inches from hers. "You were probably going to bark an order at me," he offered. His tone was lighthearted.

Lucy stepped back to escape the magnetic pull of his gaze. "Why, ah…why don't you find a tree to tie that rope to?" she whispered.

Eli unrolled the rope and glanced up and down the bank. "Wouldn't it make more sense to find a bridge and pull the boat out that way, so we don't have to cross the river?"

Time was of the essence. Why was he trying to change the plan? "The bridge is five miles away on rough road. This is the best way to do it." She pointed at a tree about ten feet upriver. "That one looks strong enough."

He darted to the tree and secured the rope. She liked the way so little instruction was required for them to get this job done...once he stopped arguing with her.

He trotted back toward her. "I'll go in."

She shook her head and took the rope. "I'm the one who knows this river. I'll need your strength at the other end to pull the boat across stream."

He opened his mouth and lifted his chin as if preparing to argue, but then he bent toward her and squeezed her upper arm. "Are you sure you won't take the life jacket?"

The level of concern he showed caused her heart to swell. She wasn't used to someone caring so much about her safety. "It's all the way back up at the van. We need to get this done."

He nodded.

She lunged into the water. The waders insulated her from the cold, but the beating waves nearly knocked her over. Water chugged and surged around her. At its deepest, this part of the river only came up to her waist. The strength of the waves, though, was more than she had been prepared for. She forded the river by pressing into the water, lifting her feet as little as possible.

There was something reassuring about seeing Eli on the bank, holding the other end of the rope. He stepped a few feet into the river.

The boat, wobbling from the impact of the waves, was within ten feet. The felt bottoms of her wader boots prevented her from slipping. A final lunge put her within reach of the boat. She lifted the rope to tie it to the boat. Bending her frozen fingers took a degree of effort. She tied the rope through the metal loop on the boat's bow.

The strength of the undertow vacuumed around her legs. She grabbed the rim of the boat to steady herself. She turned and signaled with her flashlight for Eli to start pulling the boat in. She shoved her flashlight into the chest pocket of the waders. Her arm muscles strained as she gripped the rim of the boat to keep it from drifting too far downriver.

Her leg muscles tired from fighting the strength of the water. She gasped for air, leaning harder against the boat than she should have.

Eli stepped farther into the river and continued to pull on the line.

The angle of the rope indicated that she had drifted some distance downriver. The current was stronger than she had anticipated. Not taking the life jacket had been foolish. She knew better. She could be so stubborn sometimes. Maybe she hadn't taken the life jacket because she didn't want Eli to be right.

She adjusted her grip on the rim of the boat and trudged forward. The water felt like marble around her legs. Her shoe slipped between two rocks and stuck. Fighting exhaustion, she struggled to free herself. She was wedged in tightly, unable to move much at all. Waves pushed against her as she angled her upper body in an effort to twist the ankle loose.

She pivoted, swayed sideways and fell into the water. Her foot broke free, but she plunged under water.

Freezing water chilled her toes and moved up her calves. In her haste, she hadn't secured the drawstring of her waders and now they filled with icy water. All this weight would make her sink like an anchor. She took in a breath that was mostly water.

She'd lost all sense of where she was. Water covered her head, surrounded her, pushed down on her face. She flailed her arms. She had to get out of these waders or she'd drown. She pushed her head above water, gasped in a breath and went under again. Her hands were like dough as she fumbled with the zipper and straps of the waders. She was so cold, even bending her fingers took effort. She broke the surface of the water to steal another breath. Dark waves battered against her head; she could see nothing else.

Again the water overwhelmed her as its weight pushed her toward the river bottom. Air, she needed air. Lucy fought off the fog that entered her mind. She had to get out of here, had to free herself. Energy drained from her body as she pressed cold fingers against one of the click-in shoulder straps.

Like lights being clicked off in a hallway, her systems were shutting down one by one. Movement, the lifting of her arms through the water, slowed. She couldn't feel her legs. Her mind could not form a thought. She reached out for what she hoped was the boat. Nothing.

She could not move her arms or her fingers. Still underwater, she lay back, drifting toward the darkness she had resisted, growing numb.

SIX

His heart pounding, Eli lifted Lucy out of the water. Her head swayed to one side and her eyes were closed. He repeated her name several times and patted her cheek. Lucy took in a ragged breath. She opened her eyes.

"There you are," he whispered.

He placed a knife underneath one of her shoulder straps and cut. She jerked slightly when the cold metal dug into her skin. Water from his hair dripped on her face. She blinked and looked at him with glazed eyes. At least she was conscious.

He cut the other strap and tried to pull the waders off by tugging downward. The water crested around them.

She was too weak and too weighed down to make it to shore, and he couldn't get her out of the waders until she was out of the water. He had to get her into the boat, but she wouldn't be able to lift her legs to climb in by herself. She swayed slightly in his arms.

He leaned close so she would hear him above the roar of the river. His lips brushed her ear. "I'm going to let go of you just for a second, so I can lift you into the boat."

Lucy nodded. Eli slipped his hand free of her waist and then grabbed her arm and draped it over his shoulder. She grabbed the rim of the boat and tumbled in while he pushed from behind.

She lay with her back against the boat, looking up at him. With his knife, Eli cut down the side of the waders and water whooshed into the boat.

Rain sprinkled against her face. Her breathing was labored. She'd been responsive to his commands, but the unfocused look in her eyes told him she was traumatized. She was dangerously close to hypothermia.

Eli jumped back into the water and guided the boat to shore. Water had matted his hair.

"We're pretty close to shore." He shouted to be heard above the clamor of the rapids. He touched a hand to her cheek. "It won't be long now."

She mouthed the words, "Thank you."

They reached the shore. After helping Lucy out of the boat, he tugged it high up on the rocky beach, where there was no danger of the waves catching it and pulling it back into the current. Lucy hadn't brought a trailer; she must have intended to retrieve the boat later.

By the time Eli guided Lucy back up to the van, she was shivering uncontrollably and slurring her words, the early signs of hypothermia. He had all but carried her up the hill. For the fourth time, Lucy had asked about the boat.

He cupped his hands on her cheeks. "The boat is fine. We need to get you dry and warm." He leaned a little closer, a gesture that forced her to look in his eyes. "You need to get out of those wet clothes. Do you understand me?" He punctuated each word, hoping she was not beyond understanding his instructions.

She blinked several times before nodding.

He opened the back end of the van, searching through the boxes of supplies until he found a shirt and pair of pants. "This is the best equipped vehicle I ever saw."

"My clients sometimes need a change of clothes." Her voice vibrated from her shivering. "They fall in the river."

Her answers were becoming more coherent, a good sign. He handed her the clothes. "You can change in the back here. I'll close the doors." Her hands were still trembling and her lips had no color. "Or do you need me to help?"

"I can do it." She had already slipped into the back of the van.

Her response probably had less to do with modesty than her wanting to do everything without help. Even in her weakened state, Lucy was fiercely independent.

He closed the back of the van and turned away. Water drops pelted his plastic raincoat. He shook his head. Lucy had forgotten to tie her own drawstring because she had helped him with his. Why hadn't he been paying more attention? He could have prevented her waders from filling with water.

He slipped out of his waders. The rest of the gear from Lucy's vehicle had served him well. Even though his clothes underneath were damp, he was cold but not frozen. The darkness of the sky indicated that the storm was going to last for some time. Lucy was still not out of danger. He had to get her home and warmed up.

When Lucy tapped on the back window, he whirled around and stalked back to the van. He swung the doors open. Lucy had almost no color in her face. He masked the panic he felt and steadied his voice. "How are we doing?"

"I—I—I—can't get these snapped." She held

up trembling white fingers. She'd donned the pullover flannel shirt but was struggling with the snaps on the down vest he had grabbed.

Again, he swallowed hard and managed a smile that didn't give away how concerned he was about her condition. "Let me get that for you." She gazed up at him like a child getting her winter coat fastened as he worked. He pressed the final snap at her neck. His face was inches from hers. Her breathing was shallow, slow. He touched her cold cheek with the back of his hand. "Maybe we should get you to the hospital."

She shook her head. "No, no, I'm fine."

"I don't know about that." He shone the flashlight on her face. At least her pupils weren't dilated. He set the flashlight down and grabbed her hands, enveloping them in his own. "You are shaking like a leaf."

"I've dealt with this before."

"In other people, not in yourself." Her hands were like frozen stones in his.

She laughed. The out-of-place social response told him that she still wasn't beyond total hypothermia. A thermal blanket caught his eye. He grabbed it, tore open the package it was in and unfolded the covering, which looked as if it was made out of ultrathin flexible tinfoil. He wrapped it around her.

"Please, just take me home." She tilted her head. Her blue eyes filled with vulnerability.

He brushed a strand of long hair off her face and spoke gently. "Did you leave the keys in the car?"

She nodded, shivering.

Shielding her from the rain with the blanket, he helped her into the passenger side of the van.

He started the vehicle, and it lumbered up the hill. Eli kept one eye on the road and one eye on Lucy. She slumped forward slightly. The rough road caused both of them to jiggle side to side. He could monitor her condition by keeping her talking.

"So you lived in Mountain Springs your whole life?"

"Yes." She stared at the floor of the van, her voice barely above a whisper.

Not much of an answer. He pulled up onto the smoother road. He asked her several more questions. She offered only one-word answers or no answer at all.

Eli struggled against the growing tension in his shoulders and back. Her skin was still whiter than white. "Got any family here?"

She rubbed her temple. "Grandpa and Grandma and Mom are all gone."

Minutes passed as he drove. The headlights cut a swath of illumination through the twilight.

The road curved, forcing him to concentrate on his driving. Tension squeezed his rib cage. He angled the vehicle into a tight curve. In his peripheral vision, it looked as though she was slumped against the window. "So what has the fishing been like this year?" No response. He gripped the steering wheel tighter. "Lucy, I just—"

She took in a sudden breath and repositioned herself in the seat. "You just want to keep asking me questions to make sure I'm not slipping away." She lifted her head. "You know, I took first aid classes, too. I am just weak from what I went through."

Relief spread through him. Strength had returned to her voice. He reached over and squeezed her shoulder. "Back among the living."

She drew the blanket tighter around her. "Still really cold and kind of numb, but I don't feel like my brain is made of gelatin anymore."

"We'll get you warmed up." He hit the blinker and turned onto the gravel road that led to her place.

"I was stupid. I should have taken the life jacket you offered." She gathered the Mylar blanket at her neck. "I can be a little…pigheaded sometimes."

"You were just very focused on getting that boat." Mistakes had been made on both their parts. He should have insisted he be the one to go into the river. He brought the van to a stop by the duplex.

A few stars peeked out from behind the storm clouds as the rain fell. While she fumbled with her seat belt, he got out and raced to the passenger side. He opened the door, stepped up on the sideboard, reached across her and undid the seat belt. Her face brushed against his chest as he straightened his back. He held out a steadying hand. To his surprise, she didn't protest. She took his hand and jumped down from the van seat. She wobbled. He placed a supportive arm around her waist and helped her up the stairs to the porch.

He lifted the keychain he'd pulled from the car. "One of these opens your door?"

She nodded, and he placed the keys in her open palm. "I never used to have to lock my doors until the robbery." She found the right key, but fumbled when she tried to place it in the keyhole.

His hand grazed the silky surface of her palm as he took the key and twisted it in the lock.

"Guess I'm still kind of shaky. My fingers are really stiff," she said.

Was that embarrassment he heard in her voice? "You've been through a lot. You don't need to feel bad about needing help." He pushed the door open, allowing her to walk by herself.

"I'm cold." She rubbed her forearms.

"You know not to get into a hot bath or just

warm your limbs." He turned a half circle in the living room.

"I had that survival training, too, remember." She collapsed on the couch. "I know I have to get my core warmed up. Internal body temp has probably dropped a couple degrees. Blah, blah, blah."

Eli chuckled. Despite the weakness of her voice, there was a little bit of that sassy, defiant Lucy in her remark, the part of her he was starting to like quite a bit.

She locked him in her gaze. "What are you smiling about?"

"Nothing. I'm glad you're feeling well enough to argue with me."

He found a space heater and a blanket and brought them back into the living room. He studied her as she wrapped the blanket around herself. She lifted her head. He shifted in the chair. "We had a little bit of a scare there, huh?"

"A little one." She peered at him with those blue eyes.

Even as they spoke, he could feel the walls going up around her. Why was she so afraid to be vulnerable? "You going to be okay?"

"I'll be fine," she said curtly.

Impulsively, he breached the short distance between the couch and chair. He touched two fingers to her neck. She didn't draw back from him. Their heads touched.

"I think it is okay," she whispered.

His fingers lingered on her neck. He breathed in her sweet scent. He longed to kiss her.

He pulled his hand away from her neck. What was he doing? He scooted back to the couch. "Heart rate feels normal." He swallowed to get the lump out of his throat. He'd be lying to himself if he said his action had been purely for medical reasons. Lucy Kimbol was getting to him, which made no sense at all, since she was the most guarded woman he had ever met.

He rose to his feet and paced. Now his heart was racing. "All the same, I might give you a call a couple times tonight." He was talking a mile a minute. Stunned by the power of his attraction to her, he strode to the door.

She followed him with the blanket still around her shoulders. "Eli, thank you." She stood about two feet from him. "My friends all say I'm not very good at asking people for help. Sometimes it's nice to just have someone who gives it without being asked."

His hand twisted the doorknob. She'd called him Eli. The sound of his name on her lips caused heat to rise up in his face. "Is that what I did?"

She nodded, tilting her head, eyes clear and vulnerable again.

He couldn't bring himself to look at her. Afraid the lingering smolder of emotion might ignite. He swung the door open and stepped out onto the porch. He was just in Mountain Springs to do a job, to catch a killer, to prevent any more deaths…to keep Lucy safe. He'd be leaving when the job was done; emotional entanglements were a bad idea.

Lucy had followed him out onto the porch. Her proximity made his skin tingle.

She hugged herself for warmth. "Maybe we should go and look for my fly rod at the pawnshops. I'm sorry I dismissed the idea."

"I gotta work tomorrow." The porch light washed over her, warming her skin to a golden tone. Her parted lips and long neck enticed him. He could not bring himself to say no to her. "Maybe late in the day."

"That will work. I'll be taking some clients out on the river for a half-day workshop." She stepped toward him. "I'll knock on your door when I get back."

The energy of attraction was like warm honey underneath his skin. He reached up to touch her cheek. His fingers electrified with blue heat.

"The color's returning to your skin." His reason for touching her had nothing to do with her medical condition.

She leaned into his touch. "Am I going to make it?"

He drew back. It was wrong to play these games with a woman's heart when his own emotions had taken him by surprise. He stepped away from her. "You'll be just fine," he said in the best clinical tone he could manage. He needed to be alone, to sort through things.

His boots pounded on the wood of the porch as he made his way to his door. Lucy was still standing beneath the light, looking beautiful with the silver sheath around her, when he slipped into his side of the duplex.

Eli closed the door and leaned against it. He wasn't going to be able to sleep. He did some push-ups, made himself a snack and then reviewed the files from the case. He combed through the photos of men and women holding hands, sitting with heads close together at restaurant tables, going into movie theaters. He slammed the file shut. Not what he wanted to think about right now.

He sat down in his living-room chair and kicked off his wet boots. The storm still raged outside, rattling the windows. Even the thought of Lucy made his heart rate speed up. He crossed his arms over his chest and stared at the wall. The hypnotic rhythm of the rain lulled him. Eventually, his head fell forward and he slept.

He jerked awake. His watch said it was midnight. He had promised Lucy he would call her. He doubted there was any danger of her slipping into unconsciousness. Even as he pressed the numbers on the phone, he knew it was just an excuse to hear her voice.

When she didn't pick up on the fifth ring, panic flooded through him all over again. He let it ring several more times before hanging up. He read some e-mails, paced and tried calling her again. Still no answer. The phone was right there by the couch. Even if she had fallen asleep, it would have woken her up by now.

He looked at the darkness outside. A car could have pulled up while he was sleeping and he wouldn't have heard it. Someone could park on the road just beyond the forest and walk in, just as the thief had done that night.

He swung his door open and stomped barefoot across the porch. Through the window, his could see the couch and the blanket, but no Lucy. He scanned the area around her house. Nothing.

Eli pounded hard on the door. Feeling a rising

sense of danger, he thought about breaking down the door.

Just as he was about to put his shoulder full force into the door, it swung open. Lucy stood there. She touched her open palm to her heart. "You scared me half to death. I saw a flash of movement by the window from the loft. I thought the thief had come back."

Now he felt stupid for his overreaction. He tipped his head toward his shoulder and shrugged. "You didn't answer your phone."

"I couldn't sleep, so I decided to tie some flies and get some paperwork done." She held up a set of headphones. "They help me focus. When you didn't call, I thought maybe you had fallen asleep."

"I dozed off." He raised his arm to rest it against one of the porch posts but missed and stumbled forward. Since when had he become such a klutz?

When he righted himself, Lucy surveyed him head to toe. "Thanks for checking on me." She stepped back across her threshold. "Maybe I will be able to sleep now."

The door eased shut. Lucy made him feel like a bumbling seventeen-year-old. This sudden attraction had blindsided him.

Eli stood waiting for the energy of the moment

to subside before he ambled back to his side of the house.

He didn't have to act on the attraction. He was headed back to Spokane when this investigation was done. A relationship would be cruel to Lucy and would make it hard for him to do his job. Lucy would just have to put him in her famous "just friends" category.

SEVEN

Lucy walked toward the pawnshop a few paces ahead of Eli. She turned, waiting for him to catch up. The navy T-shirt he wore accentuated his chest and shoulder muscles. His brown hair, with the afternoon sun creating golden highlights in it, looked soft enough to touch. Eli held the door for her, and she stepped across the threshold. A pencil-thin man with a tuft of curly brown hair and large buggy eyes stood behind the counter. He lifted his head when the bell dinged. Recognition spread across his face.

"Lucy, good to see you."

"Hey, Robert." Lucy made her way past a display of video games.

She'd had a night to think about Eli. He had nothing to do with the Mountain Springs Police Department and what had happened with her brother four years ago. She had let her past experience cloud her view of him. His willingness to help her and pull her out of the river spoke volumes about what kind of person he was.

Robert placed a trombone in its case and snapped it shut. "How has your spring been going? Fish bitin'?"

"It's not the fish I need to bite, it's the clients." Lucy lifted a fly rod off the wall where it was leaning along with an assortment of nets and poles. "I'm managing to keep the bills paid at least."

"You lookin' for some more rods for your students? Got a nice batch of them from a widow who cleaned out her garage a while ago." Robert stepped to the end of the counter.

Lucy placed the fly rod back against the wall. "No, that's not why we're here."

Creases formed on Robert's forehead as he watched Eli wander around the pawnshop. Staring at people who were not locals was the hobby of every Mountain Springs native, but Lucy worried that it would be disconcerting to Eli. "Robert, this is Officer Eli Hawkins. He's renting the other side of my duplex. He's helping me look for some items that got stolen from my place."

Robert rubbed under his chin, which drew attention to his large Adam's apple. "I heard about that." He placed the trombone case on a shelf behind him. "What got stolen?"

Lucy described each item that had been taken. Even talking about the jewelry caused her spirits to drop. "It was mostly costume jewelry. My grandmother's ring did have a small ruby in it. Maybe the thief grabbed them because they looked like they were worth something."

Eli crossed his arms and rested them on the glass of the jewelry case. "I don't see anything remotely close to what you described."

Lucy edged toward him and stared into the case. She scanned each piece of jewelry, and then stood up straight. She strained to keep the disappointment out of her voice. "It was a long shot, anyway."

Eli clamped a supportive hand on her shoulder. "Don't give up so easy. This is only the first pawnshop we've come to."

Robert leaned on the counter. "Your bamboo rod got stolen, too, huh?"

Lucy nodded.

"That was such a unique rod." Robert grabbed the glass cleaner from a shelf behind him. "A thief would be stupid to try and pawn it anyplace close to where it was stolen. I know I would recognize the engraved handle."

"I suppose you're right." Her voice broke. Maybe they would recover the fly rod, but she doubted they'd find the jewelry. It was the jewelry that mattered more to her. Those few simple pieces were her connection to the past and to the people who had loved her. "The robber probably threw the earrings and other things in a trash can when he realized they weren't worth anything."

"You never know." Robert shrugged. "Sometimes people come in here, and they think something is really valuable when it isn't or vice versa."

Maybe there was still hope. "Grandma's wedding ring was pretty simple, but it must have had some value. I wrote up a description of everything. I can get that to you."

"That would be good. I promise I'll keep a lookout for you." Robert sprayed the glass cleaner where Lucy and Eli had touched and wiped it clean with a cloth he had in his back pocket. "I know a guy who works at a pawnshop up to Wilson. I can give him a call."

Robert's kindness touched her. "Thank you. Don't put yourself out, but if you do come across anything, let me know."

Music from a nearby park streamed through an open window. The jazzy tune cheered Lucy. The arts festival must be getting underway already.

Eli ambled around the store, stopping to examine the hunting rifles. "Are there any other stores around here that sell used sporting goods?"

The festival music swelled to a crescendo. Lucy stepped toward Eli. "Sure, there are at least five towns within a couple hours' drive of here. You're not thinking about checking all of those?"

"That's how police work is done," Eli said. "So glamorous, right?"

But Eli was helping with this search on his off-duty hours. "I hate to take up so much of your free time."

He turned toward her and met her gaze. "I don't mind, really, Lucy." He tilted his head toward the window. "Where is that music coming from?"

"The arts-and-crafts festival over in the park." Robert lifted a box of DVDs off the floor, scooted out from behind the counter and slipped the movies into slots on a display shelf. "I saw Dawson setting up his booth a while ago."

"Who's Dawson?" Eli glanced toward her, eyes searching.

Lucy's back muscles pinched. Eli didn't need to know everything about her.

Robert slapped a DVD on the counter. "Lucy's brother. You haven't met him yet?" He stopped shelving the movies and directed his comment to Eli. "Dawson Kimbol is a world-class wood sculptor. He does beautiful work. Lucy, why have you been keeping your brother a secret?"

"I wasn't keeping him a secret. We have plans to go fishing while he's in town." Lucy fought to keep the emotion out of her voice. Even as she spoke, anxiety rose up in her. She was proud of her brother, of what he had accomplished, but Eli's way of gently barging into her personal life made her feel exposed. "I barely know Detective Hawkins. I'm not going to tell him my whole life story." She stepped toward a rack of leather coats and pretended to be interested in a blue one with fringe.

Why do my defenses go up so easily around him?

"A festival, huh?" Eli angled his head so Lucy would look at him. "I like celebrations." He stepped toward the rack of leather jackets.

"You guys should go on over there. Lots of good food and music," Robert offered.

"I really need to get back home." She gave Eli a steely look but felt herself weakening even as she spoke. What was it with him? He had this way of making her both afraid and excited by the prospect of spending time with him, the same heightened mixture of emotions she'd felt when she'd gone cliff gliding. "I have a lot of prep work to do."

"I don't know. I'm with Robert." Eli hooked a thumb through the belt loop of his faded Levi's. "It might be kind of fun."

"Park is only three blocks up. Get yourself a

beef pasty and homemade lemonade. They're the best." Robert gave Eli a thumbs-up sign.

Lucy glared at Eli. He responded with a grin. She hadn't noticed what an intense shade of brown his eyes were before now. No use putting up a fight. She was outnumbered. "Okay, but I only want to stay a short time. I'll introduce you to my brother and we'll go."

Lucy thanked Robert and made her way to the door. Once outside, she whirled around to face Eli. "I don't like being talked into things."

"I understand that. It's just that I'd like to meet your brother, since the way you talked about him, I thought he was dead." He looped her arm in his.

"I never said my brother was dead. My private life is my private life." Even as familiar anxiety rose to the surface, she was reminded of how safe she had felt with him last night when he had rescued her from the river. "You're kind of a buttinsky."

His eyebrows drew together. "Buttinsky? I don't think I've heard that word since seventh grade."

His lighthearted response made her feel less defensive. "Oh, quit." She punched him in the shoulder. "You're nosy. You're finding out all this stuff about me. I don't know anything about you."

"You haven't asked."

"I can ask you anything?"

Eli's bicep stiffened slightly where her arm was looped through his.

"Sure…okay," he said. He pulled free of her arm.

The music grew louder as they made their way up the street. The park had two clear sections divided by a road. One side consisted of craft booths. The other side featured tents that sold food and two visible performance areas. On one stage, the jazz band they had heard from a distance performed, and the other was a smaller stage in a grove of trees where it looked as though a Shakespeare play was going on.

Eli pointed to the row of concession tents that advertised everything from pizza slices to pulled pork. "I am starving. My treat."

"The plan was to meet my brother, remember." Lucy matched Eli's pace. The food did smell good. Maybe they would have to get something to eat. "So what about you?" They passed booths that had jewelry, hand-painted scarves and framed watercolors.

"Not much to tell. I have one older sister and one younger one. Mom is a nurse and Dad owns a car dealership."

"Sounds like you had a pretty normal childhood." Nothing like her own. Lucy had only vague memories of her father. Before the cancer diagnosis, her mother had worked so much that Lucy had been her brother's caretaker from a young age. The time she had spent with her grandfather fishing and learning the river was what had made life bearable.

Even from a distance, Lucy knew which booth was Dawson's. Carved wooden animals, everything from bears to tropical birds, populated the grassy area around the booth. Seeing the large crowd milling through, marveling at the sculpture, made Lucy's heart swell with pride. Dawson had done so well…despite…

"We'll just stay for a minute. I guess it wouldn't hurt to get something to eat, too."

Lucy made her way to the tent where Dawson sat in a wheelchair holding up an intricately carved eagle for a woman to look at. The woman took the sculpture, turning it over in her hands.

Dawson's face brightened when he saw Lucy. "Hey, big sis. Thought I wasn't going to see you until late tonight."

She leaned down and gave him a hug. "Change of plans." Memories of Dawson as a skinny teenager flashed through her mind. They'd both been so young when their world had turned upside down. It was a blessing that it was a week past her eighteenth birthday when their mother had died.

With Grandpa and Grandma already gone, Dawson could have ended up in foster care.

Dawson leaned forward and held out a hand for Eli to shake. "I'm Lucy's brother." He slanted a mischievous glance toward Lucy. "My sister is not good at introductions," he teased.

Lucy made a *tsk*ing noise. "I was going to introduce him. Dawson, this is Eli Hawkins. He is my renter." She swept her hand toward the craft booths. "I thought I would show him some Mountain Springs culture."

Dawson sat up a little straighter in his chair. "New in town, huh? What brings you to our thriving metropolis?"

Eli cleared his throat. "I just joined the Mountain Springs police."

"I heard they hired a couple of new officers." He craned his neck to face his sister. "I'm surprised that Lucy rented the place to you."

Dawson had chosen his words carefully, but any reference to the police department made her tense. In so many ways, Dawson had recovered better from the accident than she had. Her brother still struggled, but the initial anger and devastation he had expressed about the radical rerouting of his life had been transformed into creative energy.

Over and over, she had told herself she had

forgiven the police; she'd prayed about it, gone to counseling. If these old emotions were just beneath the surface, though, maybe she really hadn't worked through it. Maybe avoiding the police was a way of avoiding the emotions. She twisted the hem of her shirt. She really didn't want to think about the past.

"Eli is from Spokane." Lucy dug into the soft dirt with the heel of her shoe. "He is new to the force here."

Dawson's voice flooded with compassion. "I know that, sis." His hand stroked her forearm.

Eli rocked back and forth on his heels. "Oh, and I forgot to tell you about my second job. I am the self-appointed ambassador for the Mountain Springs Police Department." Eli squared his shoulders and flexed his biceps theatrically. He must have sensed the tension in the air. The tone of his comment was intended to lighten the moment.

Dawson threw back his head and laughed. "That's a good job for you."

Lucy crossed her arms and shook her head. She appreciated Eli's sense of humor, but what exactly had Dawson meant?

A woman sauntered over to Dawson, holding a carved horse. She stood a few feet away, waiting to ask him a question. Traffic in the booth had picked up.

"We should probably let you get back to business." Lucy ruffled her brother's hair. He was a grown man, but she couldn't help herself. No matter how old he got, he would always be her little brother. The only family she had left. "We're going to get something to eat. Can we get you anything?"

Dawson shook his head as more people came into the booth. "I got work to do."

Lucy leaned closer to her brother. "Are you sure you're not hungry? I can bring it over to you."

"You'll have to forgive my sister, Eli. She was eighteen when Mom died, and she had to take care of a rambunctious thirteen-year-old. She still likes to act like my mom."

"Oh, really?" Eli leaned toward Dawson, indicating that he wanted to hear more.

That settled it. Lucy tugged on Eli's shirtsleeve. "You're starving, remember." She led him over to the pasty booth.

When their order was up, Eli handed Lucy her pasty and a lemonade.

"It's a little quieter over there." She pointed toward a picnic table on the edge of the park beside a children's slide and swing set. They settled on top of the picnic table, facing the activity of the festival. Three children played on the slide while a mom watched from a bench.

"So was that your turning point...when your mom died?" Eli took a sip of his lemonade and set it on the table. "Is that when you became a Christian?"

The question was fair enough. She liked talking about her faith, but Lucy couldn't help but think it would lead to more questions. "Actually, I became a Christian a little bit before. By the time she finally went to the doctor, the cancer was stage four."

Even as she spoke, she realized she hadn't shared the whole story and all the emotions that went along with it with anyone. She had prayed all through her mother's illness. God had been so close to her during that time. She hadn't been alone. The older women from the church had been kind, bringing by casseroles and offering hugs, but she had never talked about her feelings. This was a small town; everybody knew everybody's business. She had never had a reason to tell anyone what was going on with her mom. "Before the diagnosis, she was always tired and kept saying she couldn't get a deep breath. I think we all saw it coming, but we just didn't want to say the word *cancer.*"

As she shared, her throat got tight and her voice

broke. All of this was such ancient history, why were these emotions coming to the surface now? Lucy angled slightly away. She tore at the paper her pasty had been wrapped in.

Eli rested a warm hand on her shoulder. She tensed. Maybe she had told him too much. With gentle pressure on her shoulder, he turned her around to face him. Compassion filled his brown eyes. "That was a lot for a kid to go through alone."

"Yeah, but I'm not a kid anymore." Her vision of him blurred. "That was ten years ago."

"Then those tears have been due for ten years."

She swiped at her eyes. "I guess they are." With anyone else she would have been apologizing and running off somewhere to cry alone, but with Eli she didn't feel the need to do that. "I didn't cry much when the whole thing was happening. I had to be strong for Dawson."

"Sometimes the emotion comes later. When you are in the middle of a firefight, you don't break down and bawl."

She hadn't thought of what she had been through as like being in a war. She sniffled. Fair was fair. He had to answer some questions, too. "So what about you? What was your turning point? I bet you came from a good Christian family—a total *Leave It to Beaver* life."

He chuckled. "I did come from a good family, but I didn't become a Christian until about four years ago."

"What happened?"

"It was a…a case we were working." Eli shook his head and stared at some unseen object in the distance. His features hardened, and he spoke in a low voice. "I looked evil in the face and knew I couldn't handle it alone."

The shift in mood was dramatic. All the levity of his personality had vaporized.

She leaned a little closer to him and whispered, "What was the case about?"

He lifted his head and grinned, but the smile didn't quite make it to his eyes. "You ordinary mortals don't need to know about those police things."

"Us ordinary mortals?"

Eli scooted away from her. "As a cop, you see so much…ugliness. Other cops understand. We share with each other." He slipped off the picnic table, scooped up the paper containers from their lunch and headed toward the trash can.

Lucy stared at the view of Eli's back. His reaction seemed almost nervous. What was that about? She'd shared her heart with him, and he'd closed up like a clam. Even Eli had secrets.

EIGHT

Eli wasn't surprised when he heard Dawson's van pull up to the house. Lucy had said he was going to stay with her and that they were going out on the river after he was done with the festival tomorrow. The knock on his door, though, made him jump.

He walked the short distance from the kitchen where he had been making a snack and swung the door open.

Dawson was on the porch. When Eli had moved in, he had noticed the ramp at one end of the porch and not thought anything about it until now. Though his hair was dark brown, Dawson had the same light skin and blue eyes as his sister. The arch of his eyebrows and his sunny mood gave him an almost elfin quality. Eli had a hard time picturing Dawson ever being sullen.

"Did you forget which side your sister lives on?"

Dawson laughed. "Nah, man, I just wanted to invite you to come fishing with us tomorrow."

"I don't think Lucy would like that." She'd been so transparent with him when they'd talked at the festival. He hadn't seen what dangerous ground he was treading on until Lucy had probed about his work. He could talk about his personal life and childhood all day long, but talking about the circumstances of the serial killer case in Spokane could have led to more questions about his work and a breach of secrecy on the case.

Dawson offered Eli a smile. "Lucy is not inviting you. I'm the one inviting you because you win the prize."

"What prize is that?" Eli rested a shoulder against the door frame.

"So far, you are the only cop to get within twenty feet of Lucy."

Now he realized he was going to have to increase that distance. He would be lying to himself if he said he wasn't attracted to Lucy. The gravitational pull toward her hadn't been entirely about keeping her safe.

Whatever his feelings, it wouldn't be fair to her to keep being evasive.

He was paid up until the end of the month. After that, if the investigation was still going on, he'd move out and find some other way to provide protection.

Still, it bothered him that she thought cops couldn't be trusted, and Dawson seemed to think he could fix that. Officer O'Bannon had been vague about the reason for the mutual animosity. He couldn't picture Lucy saying negative things about the department without good reason. If he knew the whole story, maybe there was some way he could smooth things over.

Eli pushed his shoulder off the door frame and stepped outside onto the porch. "I don't suppose you being in that chair has anything to do with why Lucy doesn't trust the Mountain Springs police?"

Dawson tapped the heel of his hand on the wheelchair arm. "Lucy is kind of a private person. I'm not going to violate her trust. She'll tell you when she's ready."

"I really don't think Lucy would want to hang out with me tomorrow." He'd seen the look on her face when he'd refused to answer her question about the serial killer case that had made him see a need for God in his life. She probably felt played after she'd been so vulnerable.

"Being in this chair isn't easy." Dawson pulled on a Velcro tab on his fingerless glove and pressed it back into place. "Every day when I wake up, I wish I had my legs back, and I think about the life I might have had. Lucy and I were going to run the guide business together. It's not easy, but I'm getting through it."

"And Lucy?"

"Lucy has had to be a grown-up since I was born. She's lost all the people she loved and nearly lost me. She's a little overprotective of me. I had to move to a different town so she would quit hovering." Dawson rolled back in his chair and touched his thigh with a fist. "The damage that was done to me is obvious. With Lucy it's deeper, more hidden."

Eli traced the pattern of the wood in the door trim. "I don't know. I think it might be better if I just stay Lucy's renter."

Dawson motioned with his hand for Eli to bend closer. "I heartily disagree, my friend." He scooted back in his chair. "We're going to meet at the river, Spanish Creek exit about a mile up, around 5:00 p.m. after the booths close up at the festival." Dawson lifted his front wheels and swung in a half circle. He turned his head and spoke over his shoulder. "I expect to see you there. I'll bring extra gear."

Eli spent the next day running surveillance on suspect number two, Neil Fender, who lived in Wilson, a town about fifty miles from Mountain

Springs. His thoughts kept wandering back to Dawson and his invitation. All afternoon he had debated about going. He found himself thinking about Lucy all the time.

William sat opposite Eli at a restaurant, reviewing the case. Two tables down, Neil Fender had just wrapped up another successful date and left the restaurant.

William poured sugar into his coffee and stirred. "You notice how Neil Fender is somebody different to every woman he dates." He set the spoon on the table. "But does that make him a killer?"

In the time they had watched Neil, he had pretended to be a hunting guide and a millionaire, and had told one woman about his tragic childhood in an orphanage. None of his stories were remotely true, but all of them made the women he dated want a second date.

"Isn't dating all about deception?" Eli flipped through a written report. "Only showing the best side of yourself?" Yet another reason he had chosen career over marriage. Courtship was so filled with land mines. The bad guys were easier to identify in his job.

"Neil Fender isn't showing the best side of himself." William took a sip of his coffee and slammed the cup on the table. "He's showing a false side."

"He's really good at reading women and saying what they want to hear. I'll give him that." Eli flipped through the photos on his laptop of Neil that showed him with his various dates. Some were blond. Some brunette. In fact, none of the suspects so far were consistently picking dark-haired, blue-eyed women, which made him wonder if they were on the wrong track. "I really don't think Neil Fender is anything more than a sleazebag. I feel like we are wasting time and manpower."

"Could you use some good news?" William rested his elbows on the table and leaned closer to Eli. "Officer Smith has managed to snag a date with Greg Jackson."

"Good. I still think Jackson is our strongest suspect." Jillian Smith had proven herself to be quite adept at undercover work. At least that part of the case was moving forward. "She has been well-prepped. Hopefully, her line of questioning will push Jackson to reveal something that will allow us to obtain search warrants, maybe even bring him in for questioning. If we can get a search warrant, we might find something in his place that links him to the deaths." If. If. If. Eli clenched his teeth. The longer they were stalled, the less likely they would find anything.

William doodled on a cover page of one of the reports. "We have been focused on means and opportunity with this guy—what about motive?"

Eli enjoyed the feeling of the late-afternoon sun streaming through the window. He should be outside, maybe on a river with a beautiful woman. He smiled at the thought and refocused his attention on William. "We might not know that until we make the arrest."

"Maybe he was hurt by a dark-haired and blue-eyed woman. Maybe his mother had dark hair and blue eyes and she was horrible to him."

"It's not usually that straightforward. All the same." Eli clicked through files on his laptop; he turned the screen so William could see the photograph of Greg Jackson's mother. A large man in coveralls stood behind her, his hand resting possessively on her shoulder. His scrunched eyebrows and cold eyes communicated inflexibility. It wasn't a great picture, but the woman with a weary expression had dark hair. A grainy enlargement of the photograph showed that her eyes were blue.

William shook his head. "Jackson has a lot of key personality indicators. You said he seems pretty tightly wound. Do you think we should watch him closer?"

It was a tough choice. What if they pulled the attention away from the other three suspects and another woman died? At the same time, they didn't have the funds to spend months and months watching men take women to the movies. With the case in Spokane, the killer had messed up while under surveillance. He'd had a victim's shoe in his car, and it had fallen out while he was being watched. They needed that kind of break in this case. Eli rubbed the stubble on his face. "There has to be something we're not seeing here."

Eli examined a hard copy of the file. The murders had taken place over a year and a half. The first murder had been Easter weekend in April of the previous year. Murders had occurred on different days of the week in August, October and December. The final murder had been in February. Time of death was always set between dinner and evening, date time for most people. Eli studied the map of where the murders had taken place. The varied methods of murder suggested that although there was planning in waiting for a time when he was alone with the victim, the killer tended to use whatever weapon was available. The two poisonings had been with materials found in the victims' homes. One woman had been stabbed with her own kitchen knife, and the other two strangled with a curtain cord and a dog leash.

Eli rubbed his eyes. He was so buried in the details of the case he couldn't see the big picture anymore.

He studied the place mat on the table, a picture of a man holding a large fish with the mountains and river in the background. He checked his watch. Four o'clock.

"You got some place you need to be?"

"I had a fishing invitation." The drive from Wilson to Mountain Springs was less than an hour. He could still make it to the dock by five. He wanted to see Lucy one more time. Maybe he could get the ball rolling on fixing things between her and the police. He could at least do that for her, without getting tangled up in her life.

William sat back in his chair. "I don't suppose this has anything to do with a pretty, dark-haired lady?"

"She is beautiful, and I am still concerned for her safety. Don't worry, I'm not going to let it get personal."

William crossed his arms and raised an eyebrow. "Too bad the circumstances of your meeting weren't a little different, huh?"

William had voiced a thought that had run

through Eli's mind a thousand times. "There is just something I need to resolve for her."

"You are not required to work 24/7." William tossed a sugar packet at him. "Why don't you go have some fun? Make it look like you're becoming more a part of the community."

As he rose to his feet, Eli clarified the plan of action. "Let's prep Officer Smith even more before her big date. Maybe we can bring in a forensic psychologist to fine-tune the line of questioning that might get Jackson to reveal things."

"Sounds good." William stood up and stretched. "Smith has picked the date location, so we can get A/V in place ahead of time."

The drive from Wilson to Mountain Springs went by quickly on the straight road. As he pulled into the flat gravel area that served as a parking lot by the fishing access, he'd come to a clear conclusion. Lucy had been hurt enough by his need for secrecy. If he couldn't share fully with her who he was, he needed to keep his distance.

Even as he made his way toward the dock, he noticed Lucy's spine straighten. No surprise there.

A woman he assumed was her friend Heather sat cross-legged on the dock, staring at a laptop screen. Nelson positioned himself beside her, holding an open tackle box. The gel on Nelson's wavy hair caused it to take on a bright sheen in the late-afternoon sun. His clothes looked almost too new for the river. Dawson and Lucy huddled on the shore, untangling fishing line.

As he watched Lucy from a distance, his resolve weakened. Being with her felt so right.

When Eli got within earshot of the group, he heard Dawson say, "I invited him." The look of hopeful expectation on Dawson's face cut right through Eli. The guy just wanted his sister to find some healing for all the pain of the past.

Lucy shot her brother a stern look, but managed a smile for Eli. She rose to her feet and placed a hand on her hip. "Extra gear is right there."

Eli picked up a fly rod.

"Have you ever been fly fishing, Eli?" Lucy grabbed a pair of hip waders and slipped into them.

"My dad took me when I was a kid. We used a spinning thing that made noise."

"You used a lure." Lucy pulled flies from a tiny box and stuck them in her hat. "That's a different kind of fishing."

"Spin casting is for Neanderthals." Dawson raised his arms theatrically. "Fly fishing is an art form, and Lucy is the painter of masterpieces."

Heather pointed to a picture on her laptop. "What about this guy? He just lives in Wilson."

Lucy came up on the dock to look at what Heather had found. "There is no Internet connection out here. Did you save these files or something?"

When Heather nodded, her ponytail bobbed up and down. "Just trying to get the ball rolling on your future."

Eli positioned himself so he could see the screen, which revealed a picture of the charming and deceptive Neil Fender.

"It says he's a Christian and he likes the outdoors," Heather offered.

"I don't want to do that online stuff anymore. There has to be chemistry between a man and a woman. You can't find chemistry with e-mail exchanges and reading profiles."

Heather sighed and tilted her head toward the sky. "How are you going to know if there is chemistry unless you meet this guy?"

"I gave Greg three dates…nothing."

"Lucy's running out of space in her life to put the guys who are just friends, Heather," Nelson teased as he rose to his feet.

Lucy tossed her hat on the dock. "Would you two stop?"

Eli picked up Lucy's hat and handed it to her. "I agree with Lucy." He'd do anything to keep her away from Neil Fender.

"Thank you, Eli." Lucy's glowing expression as she took the hat communicated that she appreciated his support.

"I think she has a full life." He pointed to the picture on the laptop. "Besides, this Neil guy looks like a real deceiver."

"What makes you say that?" The defensiveness had crept back into her voice.

Once again, he had pushed it too far. Of course, the comment had made it seem like he was trying to run her life. She had seemed willing to let go of his weirdness in his interference with Greg. He didn't need to add fuel to that fire and rev up her suspicions again.

Eli leaned a little closer to the computer and scanned the profile. "Do you really want to date someone who sounds that perfect? Makes you wonder what he is hiding." He spoke out of the side of his mouth in a tough-guy conspiratorial tone. "He's probably unemployed and lives in his mom's basement."

I'm only trying to protect you, Lucy.

Lucy's blue eyes twinkled when she smiled. "I agree. Everyone tries to say the best things about themselves. That's why I don't think it is a good way to meet people." Lucy put her hat on and picked up a cylindrical canister that must have contained a fishing rod.

"Maybe you should give up dating altogether." Nelson wandered toward the river. "Just hang out with your friends."

"Fine, we don't have to do the online thing." Heather closed her laptop and rose to her feet. She walked past Eli, sizing him up. She was a short woman. Her eyes had a clearness to them that could be disconcerting. "I think Dawson and I should go out in the boat."

Dawson slapped his leg. "That's a great idea, Heather."

"But I thought…" Lucy glanced from Heather to Eli. Her stare sent a charge of heat through him.

"Eli has never fly fished." Dawson lined his wheelchair up with the boat.

Lucy crossed her arms. "Why don't *you* give him a basic lesson?"

"It's a lot easier for me to cast from the boat. I don't get that much of a chance to go fishing anymore. You are the best teacher."

"Looks like it has already been decided then." Eli hadn't failed to notice the conspiratorial signals that passed between Dawson and Heather.

Heather held the boat steady so Dawson could transfer from wheelchair to boat. Without a word,

Lucy raced over to her brother and helped him position his legs in the boat first. Then she slipped her arms under his armpits to move his upper body.

Eli stepped forward. "I'll help you push off." His shoulder brushed against Lucy's.

Heather grabbed Lucy's cell phone from its case on her belt and held it up. "Smile for the camera, you two." She clicked, handed the camera back to Lucy and winked at her.

Lucy and Eli exchanged a what-was-that-about look.

Heather placed the gear in the bottom of the boat and hopped in as soon as it began to drift. She waved at the two of them as the boat traveled downriver. "Have fun."

Eli shook his head. Someone was doing a little matchmaking. "They seem like good friends."

"They are. I got to know Heather when she was Dawson's physical therapist." Lucy shaded her eyes. Nelson had worked his way downriver about a hundred yards. She turned to face Eli. "Ready for your first lesson?"

"I am ready to learn from a master."

The smile gracing her lips warmed his heart. "Okay, then." She picked up a rod and handed it to him. "Your first lesson is establishing a comfortable grip." She angled the handle of the rod toward him.

He wrapped his hands around the spongy handle. "Are you a golfer?"

"No, why?" It shouldn't matter whether she was cold to him or not, but it did. If something as small as her smile could elevate his spirits, he was acutely tuned in to her mood changes.

"There are three basic grips." She stepped toward him. "The way you naturally held the handle is called the golf grip. Lift the rod. Does the grip feel comfortable?"

"Not really. What are my other options?"

She repositioned his fingers so his index finger rested across the top of the handle of the pole. "That's point grip."

"No, that doesn't feel right." He had a hard time focusing on what she was saying about his thumb and third finger when her smooth, cool hand brushed over his.

"Eli, are you listening?"

"What?"

Her shoulder touched his as she gripped his hand and readjusted his finger. "Rest your thumb on the top of the rod."

He bounced the pole up and down. "Guess I can live with that." The sun warming his neck and back relaxed him. "Now do I get to go in the water? There aren't many fish out here on the beach."

His joke produced another smile. "You earn the privilege of getting in the river by showing me you can get your cast right consistently."

Eli's mouth dropped open. "You are a tough teacher."

"Fish really aren't going to be bitin' strong for another hour or so. You have time to practice. What you want to do when you cast is imitate a fly coming to feed on the water. We'll start you out with a dry fly, one that skirts the top of the water. Let me see what your cast looks like."

Eli lifted his arm and flung the line out. He turned toward her for feedback.

The sun brought out the dark brown highlights in Lucy's black hair. Her eyes looked like they were made of crystal. She pursed her lips, then tapped her finger on her chin. "That fly was dead when it hit the water. You would have had too much drag on your line. No fish would be interested."

"Are you this mean to all your students?"

"Only the ones that talk my brother into inviting them." Her tone was playful.

"I assure you, it was entirely his idea. He likes my second job as ambassador for the Mountain Springs Police Department."

As though a cloud had passed overhead, her

expression darkened. "That job probably doesn't pay very well." She stared at the water.

"I get to be with you on the river—payment enough." If this was going to be the last time he would be this close to her, he might as well enjoy it.

She lifted her head. "Why don't we work on your cast?" She edged toward him, standing close enough for him to smell the floral scent of her perfume. "There are two parts to a cast, back cast and forward cast. You control your line based on what you do with your rod. Strip out some of your line with your free hand. Lift your pole until it almost passes your ear." She pressed her fingers into his forearm. "Elbow down."

His tricep muscle strained from holding it in one place. "How long do I have to stay like this?"

She pressed a little harder on his forearm. "I just want you to be aware of where your line is before you do your forward cast. You're not focused."

It was hard to pay attention when all he could think about was how nice she smelled. "The fish are getting away."

"Eli," she reprimanded before she let off the pressure on his arm. "Now, start over. If twelve o'clock is right above you, stop your back cast at ten o'clock. Stop your forward cast at two o'clock, just past your shoulder. Keep your wrist tight the whole time."

He let the line go as she had instructed. "How was that?"

She placed her hands on her hips. "Not bad. Practice on shore a few more times." She waded out into the water. "When you are ready to come into the water, put those hip waders on." She cast a couple of times, describing what she was doing. Her line zinged through the air. The murmuring hum of the river had a calming effect on him.

Being with Lucy didn't hurt, either. Was he going to be able to disconnect from her? She hadn't brought up questions about his work. Still, it was only a matter of time.

Lucy pointed out the best places to catch fish. "Look for smooth water areas around rocks and logs." She cast again. Her line looped through the air with the grace of a ballet dancer and landed delicately on the water. The corners of her mouth curved up and her expression was the serenest he had ever seen. She was a woman in her element, as if the river was merely an extension of her.

After slipping into hip waders, Eli stepped into the river. The water was so clear he could see the rocks. He worked his way toward her in water that was just above his knees. The river took on a silver sheen where the tiny waves crested.

He could see Nelson a ways downriver, but the boat with Heather and Dawson had drifted around a bend. He stood beside her. "It's nice here, isn't it?"

"I think it's pretty special," she whispered. "I love worship on Sunday morning in church, but some of my best conversations with God happen out here."

"I can see that. God's creation makes us understand him better, like it says in Romans." He turned to face her. She tilted her head. The sunlight backlit her hair. Her cheeks flushed with color. Her lips were full and inviting.

I could just kiss her now.

He took a step back and lifted his fly rod. What was he thinking? Kissing her would be cruel, misleading.

"I wasn't thrilled when you showed up, but now I'm glad that my brother invited you. What exactly did he say?"

"He didn't tell me what went on between him and the police. He said you would tell me when you were ready."

Lucy cast her line in the water. She pressed her lips together and angled slightly away from him. "What happened four years ago between the police and my brother has nothing to do with you,

Eli. Besides, the whole thing is complicated. It goes further back than Dawson's accident. Back to high school." She drew her fishing line in. "I don't dislike all cops. You have nothing to do with what happened. I know you are a good cop."

The revelation warmed him. He still had to believe he could make things better between her and the rest of the department. "Wish you felt that way about the other guys on the force."

She still didn't face him when she spoke. "I thought they would be there to help me more than once, and each time I was disappointed. The last time, my brother ended up in a chair." Her voice had an edge to it. While a soft breeze rustled through the cottonwoods along the shore, she cast her line several more times.

He dropped his hand to his side, awed by how she cast so beautifully. "How do you get your line to curve like that?" Her emotion was still so raw; somehow, the smart move seemed to be to change the subject.

She laughed. "Practice. Which is what you should be doing."

"Yes, ma'am," Eli saluted. He waded upstream. The water rushing and whooshing around him had a hypnotic effect. Now he understood the appeal of being out on the river. No wonder Lucy loved it so much. Imitating what he had seen Lucy do, he attempted to cast. The fly splatted on the water. Behind him, Lucy giggled.

He turned back to face her. "Is that how you motivate? By laughing at your students?" He pushed through the rippling water so he was closer to her.

She reeled in her line and cast several more times.

He swallowed and chose his words carefully. "Tell me what happened, Lucy. What went on between your brother and the police?"

Her arms went limp as her line dragged in the water. She bit her lower lip. "Four years ago, Dawson was helping a youth pastor at our church. He was thinking about becoming a pastor himself." Her voice broke. She waded back through the water to the shore, where she flipped open the tackle box.

Eli followed her to the rocky beach. It was up to her how much she wanted to tell him. If she shared, he might be able to help her, but if she chose not to, he'd let it go.

She reached up toward him. "Hand me your rod. I want to change your fly to something a little heavier."

He sat down beside her while she removed the fly he'd been using. While she selected a different fly and attached it, she continued. "One of the kids Dawson was mentoring stopped coming to the youth group. The boy listed his address as a house just outside of town." She took in a breath. "I don't think Dawson quite understood what he was getting himself into. He didn't know it was a meth house...nobody did."

Eli placed a supportive hand on her back.

Lucy shook her head. "He went out to the house thinking he would just check on the kid. But when he got out there, something didn't feel right. There was no one around, but the door was open and water was boiling on the stove, like people had run and hidden somewhere." Lucy squeezed her eyes shut. "So he called me and said if I didn't hear from him in twenty minutes, I should call the police." Lucy exhaled a shuddering breath. "Dawson didn't want to panic unnecessarily. I had a feeling, though. I called the police right away."

Eli leaned closer to her. This was probably the first time she had shared the whole story.

"He was on the way back to his car. One of the drug dealers jumped him. Dawson got away. He ran into the trees, the guy went after him." She shook her fist at the sky. "Dawson dodged the guy long enough for the cops to have gotten there, but they didn't believe me that he was in danger. They didn't show up until after the dealer shot Dawson."

She sat with her knees pulled toward her chest, eyes closed, head bent. A tear slipped out from beneath her lid. Eli reached up and brushed the moisture away from her temple.

She folded into his arms and buried her face in his chest. Though she was silent, her quivering shoulders indicated that she was crying. His heart ached for her. She'd lived a lifetime of pain and had to go through so much of it alone.

After a few minutes, she pulled away and wiped her eyes. "Of course, they tried to cover it up, said that they went out there right away. But I knew better. They were ignoring me on purpose to punish me for something that happened a long time ago. I was really angry. I wrote some letters to the editor, made some phone calls. We filed a lawsuit to get Dawson's medical expenses covered. The chief of police was fired, but the other cops just kept working there. They agreed to seek funding to step up the fight against meth. None of that gets my brother out of that chair."

Eli lifted Lucy's chin. He wanted to delve further but knew this was not the time. "What they did was not right. A good cop would have responded immediately." Anger burned inside him for what she had endured. No wonder she didn't trust them. He still wondered why they didn't trust her.

Her eyes searched his. "Thank you."

"Catch anything?" A voice boomed behind them.

Eli pulled away. He'd been so tuned in to Lucy, he hadn't heard Nelson come up to them.

Nelson held up a fish in his net. Though obviously losing strength, the fish flipped side to side, causing the mesh of the net to wiggle. "I caught a good-size one."

Lucy scooted away from Eli. Color rose up in her cheeks as she bent her head and covered her face with her hair. Being caught in a moment of vulnerability had embarrassed her.

Lucy stood up, brushing sand off her back and legs. "At least somebody caught something."

Nelson pulled the fish from the net by looping his finger through its gills. He sat down beside Eli. The expansion and compression of the gills lessened and then they ceased moving altogether. "I'm going to have a nice dinner tonight."

Lucy came up behind the two men and rested a hand on Eli's shoulder.

Even as he welcomed her touch, Eli knew he could not hope for more. He had broken through her walls for one beautiful moment, but he could give her nothing in return. With his heart aching for her and for what couldn't be, he slipped free of her hand.

NINE

Lucy flipped the light switch in her living room, but the room remained dark. She worked the switch up and down. "Something is wrong with the light." She turned a half circle at the entrance of her house.

Eli came up behind her. "Electricity out?"

"I'm not sure, it might just be the bulb." Having Eli close calmed her. They had had a good day together.

After they'd finished fishing, the four of them had decided to go out to eat, all except Nelson, who had caught his dinner. As they had wandered through downtown Mountain Springs and into the park where a final festival concert was taking place, Lucy had vacillated between feeling as though she had told Eli too much and knowing that it was the right thing to do. This was all so new to her, feeling safe enough with someone to share.

Eli brushed past her and leaned into her living

room. "It's darker than a cave in there. Do you want me to go get a flashlight? I know right where one is."

"That would be good. I think all my flashlights are in the van." It was nice to have Eli next door. Dawson had already made plans to drive back to his home.

Eli's footsteps pounded on the porch floorboards, fading slowly.

Lucy stepped into her place. The light over the stove, which she always kept on, was not working, either. That meant it wasn't a bulb. Her heartbeat quickened in response to the darkness. She'd been jittery since the break-in, and the lack of light didn't do anything to calm her nerves.

She had candles and a lighter in a kitchen drawer. Those would be easy enough to find. She made her way across the living room. Her feet bumped against a laundry basket. She'd forgotten about leaving that there. Her hand brushed over the sleek wall between kitchen and living room. She entered the kitchen, counting drawers by touching the metal handles.

As she slid the third drawer open, she heard a muffled click on the other side of the room. "Eli?"

Lucy held her breath and listened. Even though her eyes had begun to adjust to the darkness, she could make out almost nothing in the room, only vague outlines of furniture. A little light from the moon filtered through the windows. Out of habit, she had closed the door when she'd stepped inside.

She turned slowly, brushing her fingers over the items in the kitchen drawer. She recognized the waxy texture of the candles right away, but nothing felt like a lighter. Her hand touched several hard square objects, chargers for something she either no longer owned or couldn't find.

Had she left the lighter by the fireplace or outside by the barbecue? Gripping the candles, she opened another drawer and felt around, lifting objects and tossing them back in. Again, she thought she heard a noise coming from the living room.

As she walked back into the living room, her soft-soled shoes were nearly silent on the wood floor. She could make out the outline of the coat tree by the door. A lump swelled in her throat. "Eli," she whispered, knowing even then that he wasn't in the room.

She stood frozen for a moment waiting for another sound, anything to verify that she wasn't imagining things. The last time she'd had a soak in the tub after a long cold day on the river, she had lit the lavender candles. She'd probably left the lighter in the bathroom.

Lucy shook off the feeling that there was someone else in the room. Darkness had a tendency to accelerate the imagination. She placed a hand on the textured wall and inched toward the bathroom. She patted her hands over objects in the medicine cabinet until she found the lighter. As she struggled to produce a flame with the lighter, she heard a thud in the living room and something scraping across the floor. Her head shot up. Her heart hammered in her chest. That was not her imagination.

The last home invasion was still fresh in her mind. She had to get out.

She flicked the lighter one more time. The candle wick caught the flame. She slipped out of the bathroom and edged back toward the living room, toward the door, toward where Eli was. In the small circle of illumination, she could see nothing out of place.

She darted the final yard across the living-room floor. Her hand wrapped around the knob; it didn't budge. Someone had thrown the dead bolt. She adjusted the candle so she could see the lock.

Something tightened around her neck. An unseen force pulled her back, dragged her across the floor. The candle slipped from her hand. She choked and gasped for air.

She swung side to side, trying to break free. Her fingers clawed at her neck. She recognized the silky fabric of one of her own scarves. She wheezed in air, growing light-headed. Orange pops of light filled her vision.

She had only seconds before she passed out. In her thrashing, she angled herself toward her assailant, barreling into where she thought his torso would be. He groaned. Her hand reached up. Something covered his face—a knit cap.

The suctioning around her neck let up as they both fell to the floor. Before she had her bearings, he yanked on her hair.

She screamed. Pain seared through her scalp.

She'd lost all sense of where she was in space. He pulled harder on her hair. She flailed her arms, trying to grab hold of something, anything to anchor herself. Her hand brushed the mantel of the fireplace. Framed photos spilled to the floor. Glass shattered.

Then her head slammed against the hard rock of the fireplace. More winking golden circles filled her vision. Temporary paralysis from having the wind knocked out of her invaded her limbs.

A cold hand stroked her cheek. Fingers slithered down her face to where her pulse throbbed in her neck.

* * *

Eli fumbled through the dark of his half of the duplex. He'd tried two light switches, enough to tell him that his electricity was out, as well. He'd managed to crash into a box and a chair on his way to the duffel he kept in his bedroom. It wouldn't hurt for him to keep the place a little tidier, considering how little he had accumulated. He owned half a dozen flashlights, but he knew for sure one was in the duffel.

As he felt around the bed, he remembered the way Lucy had looked at him at dinner and while they'd watched the concert. He'd seen affection in her eyes and the realization made his stomach tighten. He did not want to hurt her. All night, he had wanted to leave, but the smallest insistence from Lucy had made the word *no* impossible to say.

Heather's words to him only confirmed that he needed to tell Lucy he was moving into town even before the end of the month.

Heather had pulled him aside at the concert. "I don't think I have seen Lucy so relaxed in ages."

"She seems to be enjoying herself," Eli had said.

"I'm very protective of my friend." He towered over her by nearly a foot, yet her posture and the look of resolve on her face had made him feel as if he was the short one. "She has lost everyone she depended on. I was with her after Dawson's accident, and we thought we might lose him, too."

Heather's eyes had fixed on him with a steel-like gaze. "I want more than anything for Lucy to find someone special. It's obvious she likes you. If you are not the guy who can stay in her life and be good to her, don't be in her life at all. I don't think her heart can take any more loss."

Eli found the flashlight in his duffel with little effort. He wasn't about to cause Lucy more pain. He needed to back off, but he could still help her from a distance. Now that he knew what had happened to Dawson, he was going to have to talk to officers who had been around four years ago. He needed to find out too what O'Bannon and Lucy had meant by their references to high school.

Eli clicked on the flashlight and left the bedroom. He had no idea where the breaker box was. Lucy would know. Most duplexes had separate breaker boxes for each house. It wouldn't hurt to look in a few obvious places for the breaker box. Lucy had probably already found some kind of light of her own.

There hadn't been any storms all day, and all the other houses had had lights on as they'd driven back to the duplex. No reason to think the loss of current was anything but a fluke. He headed toward the half basement, thinking the breaker box might be there.

He stopped gripping the handrail. His heart froze. Realization entered his mind.

Eli raced up the stairs. There was no reason for the electricity to be out. Someone had thrown the breakers on purpose. Someone had been waiting for Lucy to come home and had assumed that he would be busy in his own place trying to get the lights on. He flung his door open and ran across the porch. The knob on Lucy's door turned, but the door didn't open. Dead-bolted. He placed the flashlight in his mouth and tried the door one more time with both hands. It would be futile to try to kick it in. When he peered in the window between the slit in the curtains, he couldn't see anything.

Eli ran around to the back of the house and tried the door that led directly into the kitchen. Dead-bolted, as well. This time when he peered in the window, he saw rising smoke and flames.

"Lucy!" he shouted. He slammed his weight against the door and then kicked it. Brute force was not going to get him inside. Eli whirled around, assessing what he had to work with. Maybe there was something in the tool shed.

Once inside the shed, his flashlight shone on several handsaws and a sledgehammer before he noticed the ladder. The night he had met Lucy, the intruder had slipped out of a window. He grabbed a hammer in case the window wasn't open and dragged the ladder across the yard.

When he leaned the ladder against the wall, it was higher than the window. His hand curled into a fist. Panic had muddled his thoughts. If the thief had gotten in and out without a ladder, he could, too. He pushed the ladder to one side, angry that he had lost so much time.

The thief must have boosted himself up by standing on the rock beneath the window.

Still holding the hammer, he climbed up, relieved to see that the window was open. The screen had been set to one side just like before. This time though it looked like Lucy had installed some kind of lock over the window. Battered trim indicated that the thief had beat on the window with something to get it open. He dropped the hammer on the ground.

As he crawled through the window, Eli was aware that the intruder may still be inside. In his haste, he had left his gun at his duplex. His feet landed on the carpet in Lucy's bedroom. He shone the light around the room, probing dark corners as adrenaline surged through his body. Once again, the place had been torn to pieces. Same guy as before. It had to be.

He raced into the living room. A throw blanket had fallen to the floor and caught on fire. Judging from the toxic smell in the air, the blanket wasn't made of natural fabric.

Lucy had risen to her feet. A spark of recognition crossed her features. Relief coursed through him. She swayed.

Eli lunged forward, gathering her in his arms before she fell. He kicked a chair aside. Still propping Lucy up, he clicked back the dead bolt on the front door. She was like a rag doll in his arms. The night sky twinkled with stars as he laid her on the front porch, taking a moment to touch his palm to her cheek. Though she didn't speak, gratitude flashed in her eyes.

They both coughed from inhaling the toxic fumes.

Cupping his hand over his mouth, he ran back inside and opened all the living room windows. The fire was not raging but had produced significant smoke. He ran to Lucy's bedroom and grabbed a wool blanket he'd remembered seeing. He placed the blanket on the flames and smoke. He spotted Lucy's cell phone on the counter, picked it up and dialed 911 for the fire department. Then he phoned William's cell number.

Eli grabbed another blanket from the bedroom and walked out to the porch, where Lucy rested against a supporting post. He shone his flashlight in her direction.

The look on her face told him everything he needed to know. This was not the time to ask questions, not the time to be a cop. She needed a friend.

He wrapped her in the blanket and pulled her close.

"Fire department will be here in a minute. It's going to be all right."

She tried to speak but only managed a horrible cough. When she touched her neck, he saw the dark red marks and scratches. He drew Lucy to his chest and held her. She trembled in his arms.

Rage over what had been done to her filled him. The crime had some similarity to the first robbery. Since Lucy had probably locked the doors this time, the assailant had entered and exited through the bedroom window, but this wasn't a simple robbery anymore.

This guy had been waiting for Lucy. There was premeditation in shutting off the electricity to make it harder for Lucy to escape and to keep Eli busy trying to get the electricity on in his place. Who would do this?

Lucy tilted her head. "If you hadn't been here…" Her voice was hoarse.

His jaw clenched. He should have gotten here

faster. He should never have left her alone. "Lucy, this is my fault, I—"

Lucy gripped his collar. "Please don't. I am so glad you were here."

He touched her forehead where there was a bump. "That's going to hurt."

She winced. "I think I lost consciousness, just for a moment." She cleared her throat and then her hand fluttered to her neck. "Eli, he could have killed me, but he didn't."

"I might have scared him off." The assailant had to have escaped by the window—both doors were still dead-bolted. Eli hadn't seen anyone in the field or by the shed when he'd crawled in.

Lucy shook her head. "No, he left before I heard you shouting and knocking."

"But he—" Eli touched the red marks on Lucy's neck. The guy had had opportunity to kill Lucy and had chosen not to. Was the assault intended as some kind of warning?

"I heard you pounding on the door…and then I saw the fire. I wasn't thinking clearly." She attempted to laugh, but it sounded more like a cough. "I actually had it in my head that I needed to get water to pour on the fire."

Up the road, two sets of headlights shone through the darkness. A single car followed by a fire truck came into view. "I want you to call Heather and stay with her. The fire damage isn't bad, but it smells in there, and I don't want to take a chance that—" He caught himself, not wanting to alarm her anymore. She'd been through enough for one night.

"—that he will come back." Lucy pressed the heel of her hand against her forehead. "For a third time. It was the same guy, wasn't it?" Lucy sat up a little straighter. "I'll call Heather."

The Volkswagen came to a stop, and William got out.

Lucy scooted away from Eli so he could get up. He leaned close and rested a hand on her cheek. "I must have left your cell in your house. It'll take a minute for those fumes to clear out. My place is open—go in there and use the phone." He studied her for a moment. She hadn't cried, hadn't fallen apart. That concerned him. It would be better for the emotions to come out than for her to deaden inside and pretend like the assault didn't bother her. "Are you sure you're okay?"

She nodded in short, jerking motions.

"Are you telling me a lie?"

She nodded again, and this time her eyes rimmed with tears. She stood up and fell into his arms. He held her and spoke softly into her ear. "You don't always have to be the strong one, Lucy."

She let out a gasp. "I want to believe that." When he pulled back to look at her, she wasn't sobbing, only a few tears trailed down her cheeks. He brushed one away with his finger.

She pulled back and lifted her chin in a show of feigned composure. Eli gripped Lucy's arm at the elbow and helped her up the stairs.

He waited on the porch until Lucy disappeared inside before going over to William, who instructed the firefighters to not disturb anything in the house that might be evidence.

"Why did you phone me directly?" William asked.

"I have some doubts about this police department when it comes to dealing with Lucy." Eli turned back toward the open door of Lucy's place. "Do we have a line on Greg Jackson's whereabouts?"

William's expression was grim. "He was in Mountain Springs earlier. Some kind of agriculture banquet. He took a woman he'd met from the service."

"And what time did the banquet end?"

"I know what you're thinking. This is not our guy's M.O. If it had been, you know and I know, Lucy would be dead."

The thought made Eli shudder. William had a point. Their guy didn't build up to a murder with robbery and assaults. He planned and he carried out his plan.

"This guy had time to kill her and he chose not to. All the same, I would like to know exactly where Greg Jackson was about an hour ago."

William nodded and pulled his phone from his pocket.

Eli paced while William made the call. Lucy would want to move back into her place within a few days. He couldn't blame her for that. She needed to be close to the river, close to her work. He was grateful she hadn't argued with him about not staying here tonight.

William hung up the phone. "Greg Jackson took his date home around nine and went back to a hotel."

"So we can't account for his whereabouts after that?"

William nodded.

Eli aimed the flashlight at his watch. Eleven o'clock. "Could he have gotten out here in that time?"

William shook his head. "It's possible."

Eli combed his fingers through his hair. Up to this point, he had treated Lucy's robbery as a separate crime and had thought of it as just a robbery, but now the crime was directed at Lucy.

Lucy stepped out onto the porch, crossing her arms over her chest. The color had returned to her cheeks. "Heather is on her way."

Eli moved toward her. "I want to go over your place."

Lucy took in a deep breath. "I don't think you'll find anything."

"It still might be worth it. I'll make sure we dust the breaker boxes." If he had the time and money, he could get a full forensics team out here. But without any clear link to the serial murders, he doubted he would get the okay on such an expenditure. He spoke gently. "Your room was messed up again. He may have taken something."

Even in the scant illumination provided by the flashlight, Eli read fear in Lucy's reaction.

"I'll need some things to take to Heather's, at least a toothbrush and my cosmetic bag. The fumes shouldn't be as bad now. I won't touch anything that might give you evidence."

Eli squared his shoulders. "I don't know if that's such a good idea."

"I can't survive without a toothbrush," she offered. "I'll just go in quickly and grab it."

"Okay," Eli said.

Lucy trudged up the stairs and disappeared inside.

William had already retrieved the forensics kit out of the car and taken out the camera.

"Let's just wait until she comes back out." Having Lucy watch them turn her home into a crime scene could trigger emotions unnecessarily.

Eli glanced toward the door. Maybe it wasn't such a good idea for her to go in there alone. He leapt up to the porch and followed her in. The firefighters with masks on were gathering the charred remains of the blanket and had set up a fan. Eli wrinkled his nose. The fumes were still evident, but not as strong. A breeze billowed the curtains. The lights were on again. Someone must have thrown the breaker box—so much for good fingerprints on Lucy's side.

She emerged from the hallway, holding a small floral bag. The glaze in her unfocused eyes told him what had happened.

"You looked in the bedroom, didn't you?"

She nodded. "Like picking a scab. What is my problem?" She shook her head. "I just had to peek. He took several of my favorite books. There was a gap on the shelf." Again, she touched her neck. "He must have taken that scarf, too, and some others are missing from the rack where I hang them."

Now the thief was taking personal items that were worth nothing monetarily. Their serial killer had never taken anything from his victims. The only reason Eli wanted to link the crimes was because Lucy was such a dead ringer for the other victims. He had to let go of the idea. "Lucy, do you have any idea who might want to do this?"

Her chin jerked up. She glanced at the photos and broken glass that surrounded the fireplace. "Those photos got knocked down in the struggle." Her gaze dropped, and she rubbed her bare arm. She placed a hand over her mouth when she coughed.

Was there something she wasn't telling him? Now was not the time to press her, but he had seen a flash of something when he'd asked the question. He edged closer to Lucy and glanced down at the destroyed photos. There was a recent picture of Lucy and Dawson. And one of a younger Lucy in a basketball uniform, surrounded by her teammates.

"This assault reminds me of something that happened in high school with my high school coach, but he left years ago," Lucy said.

"Lucy." Heather stood in the doorway. "I got here as fast as I could." She rushed over to her friend and escorted her out while putting a supportive arm around her shoulder.

Eli followed the two women out onto the porch. Heather led Lucy to the car. The backward glance she gave him, an expression filled with trust, crushed him.

I can't give you what you need, Lucy.

Whoever was doing this, one thing was clear. Lucy was in ongoing danger. Even if he could talk the chief into watching Lucy's home, she wouldn't accept the help. He couldn't move out.

Lucy glanced back at Eli standing on the porch. For a second time, he'd saved her life.

She got into the car. Heather clicked the key in the ignition, turned on the headlights and pressed on the gas. "You can stay in the guest room. It's full of my sewing and craft stuff, but the bed is really comfortable."

Lucy appreciated that her friend was trying to keep things light with chitchat. But Heather's clipped, nervous tone betrayed that she was upset.

Lucy laced her fingers together and rested them on her lap. "Thanks for coming out to get me." She coughed. Her throat felt gritty from breathing in the fumes.

"Thanks for calling me."

"Big step for me, huh? Asking for help." Lucy glanced out the window at the darkness.

"That's what friends do for each other."

"I'm not the big wreck I could have been. Having Eli here made it so much easier."

Heather pulled out onto the road that led into town. "It is nice to have a friend who is a cop."

Lucy cleared her throat.

"He is a friend, right?"

Warmth pooled in Lucy's chest as she took in a deep breath. "I never thought I would be saying this, but Eli is different."

"Dawson and I were talking about that. I saw you two out there on the river. The way you were with him."

"I know I put up walls, but he has a way of breaking through them."

"So what are you going to do about it?"

"This is all new for me." Lucy stared out at the dark road as the yellow lines clicked by. They had encountered no other cars so far. What would she do about Eli? She did hope their friendship would become something more. She glanced down at her hands, which were white from clenching them so tightly. "I really can't think about Eli until this whole robbery thing is resolved."

"Two robberies in less than a month," Heather said. "What do you think is going on?"

"I don't think this is about money like we first

thought. The guy keeps taking personal stuff." Lucy rubbed her bare forearms. "This whole thing feels like what happened in high school when I was being stalked. When I saw the photo of me with the basketball team, I remembered Coach Whitmore."

"Who was Coach Whitmore?"

"He was the girl's basketball coach in high school. Someone kept leaving explicit pictures in my gym and school locker. Sometimes after practice, a car followed me home." Lucy's rib cage tightened. "Then some personal things were taken from my locker…and then from my bedroom. I was pretty sure it was the coach, but when I went to the police, they didn't believe me. They investigated but said there was no evidence to support my claim." She closed her eyes and pressed her head against the back of the seat. Her history with this police department had started long before Dawson's accident. "Some of them were Coach Whitmore's drinking buddies. I think the reason the police didn't respond quickly when Dawson was shot was because of what I said about Coach Whitmore years before. They thought I was making it up."

Compassion permeated Heather's voice. "You never told me."

She'd never told anyone. The other girls on the

team had known some of the details. Their nickname for Coach Whitmore had been *the creep*. They were memories she would prefer to not revisit. At the time, her mom had been fighting for her life. "I could never prove that it was Coach Whitmore. He left town after my senior year, and the stalking stopped." She shuddered. "I had heard rumors that he was back in town. I didn't think anything of it until now."

"Lucy, this is serious. You need to find out if he has moved back here."

Lucy pressed her back against the car seat as familiar anxiety returned. "Even if he is living in Mountain Springs, the police probably won't do anything this time, either."

TEN

A tight knot formed at the base of Lucy's neck as she parked her car outside the Mountain Springs police station. She hadn't been in there since Dawson's accident. In the two days since she had gotten home from Heather's, she had hardly seen Eli at the duplex.

She jumped down from the high seat of the van and shut the door. If she couldn't catch Eli at home, she'd have to find him at work.

It had only taken a few phone calls to old high school teachers to find out that Coach Whitmore was back in town. Information Eli needed to know.

Lucy treaded up the stone walkway. A struggling hedge surrounded the squat brick building. The rest of the grounds consisted of brown grass with a few splotches of green and a flagpole.

The door flew open and two men in uniform stepped out. Officers Spitz and O'Bannon stuttered in their stride when they saw her. Chills trailed down her spine. Spitz ran a hand over his bald head as he passed her. The weight of their stares pressed on her back. She opened the door of the station.

Anxiety corseted Lucy's rib cage by the time she stepped inside a small room with a high counter. Usually the receptionist stood behind the counter, but today it was empty. Ten years ago, she'd walked through these doors as a scared teenager. Both Spitz and O'Bannon had been on the force back then, along with the chief who would later be fired, after Dawson's accident. Lucy had pushed for all of the officers to be fired.

"Yes, can I help you?" A male voice echoed in the silence.

Lucy leaned around the counter to peer inside the main office, which consisted of four desks, all empty. Where had the voice come from?

"Ah...I was looking for Eli Hawkins." She massaged the back of her neck where the knot had formed.

A uniformed officer Lucy knew as Nigel Peterson came out from behind a carrel, holding a cup of coffee. Lucy clutched her purse a little tighter to her chest. Peterson had been one of the officers on the force when Dawson had had his accident.

Peterson placed his coffee cup on the top of

a file cabinet. "He's out on a call. What can I help you with?" He crossed his arms over his chest.

Peterson had been fresh out of the academy and only a couple of years older than Dawson when the shooting had taken place. He hadn't aged much in four years. His red hair looked a little thinner, and he had put on a few pounds.

"He's been working on my robberies. I have an idea who it might be." She only felt comfortable talking to Eli about this. "I can just come back later."

"No, wait." He took a few steps in her direction. "He's going to be gone most of the day. Why don't you tell me what is going on?"

"If you could just give him a message. He asked if I knew of anyone who might have a reason to…break into my place." Nigel was from somewhere in Montana. He hadn't been around when she was in high school. Ten years ago, she had walked through the same doors, thinking she would find help. The condescending voices of the officers, their knowing glances at each other, floated back into her memory.

"We've all been briefed on the circumstances of your robberies. I can help you," he coaxed.

Would he even believe her? Her hands sweated as she readjusted her purse. He seemed sincere enough, but maybe he would act different once he was around the other officers. "His name is…George Whitmore. He used to be a coach at the high school. Years ago, I think he might have…I'm not here to point fingers. That's not my intention. It's just that Eli asked."

Nigel picked up a pad of paper and wrote down the name. He stood, pencil poised to write more.

Lucy shifted her weight from one foot to the other as the muscles in her neck turned rock hard. "There were some incidents in high school that made me think that maybe…"

Nigel put his pen and paper on the desk. His eyes searched hers. "It would be easier if I gave the information to Eli, wouldn't it?"

She nodded.

He placed his hands on his hips, let out a heavy sigh and shook his head. "Four years is a long time, isn't it, Lucy?" Sadness, not anger, colored his comment.

Nigel's freckles made him look younger than he really was. She had spent all this time blaming the whole department. He had just been a green rookie. "I'm sorry for the horrible things I said publicly about this police department. My hurt and my anger over what happened to Dawson made it hard for me to control my tongue."

"Some of what you said was well deserved. The chief needed to be fired. He's the one who allowed for that kind of do-nothing atmosphere. Dawson's accident was a wake-up call for all of us."

"Not all the officers feel the way you do."

He shrugged. "I can't help what Spitz and O'Bannon think."

"Maybe I'll just come back when Eli is here."

"No, wait." Nigel took a step toward her. "Eli had a talk with all of us a few days ago. We need to get past this."

Her breath caught. "Eli did that?"

"Why don't you let me see if I can close the file on these robberies? I can't accuse this Whitmore guy of anything, but I can do a little discreet digging."

There was nothing in Nigel's demeanor to confirm her suspicions, yet the old familiar fear that her needs would be dismissed snaked through her. "Eli will know about this?"

"Eli is pretty busy with…another investigation." He turned to face her. "Please trust that I will look into this for you."

She couldn't help the fear that happened almost automatically any time she even had to think about dealing with this police department. Lucy stopped fidgeting with her purse and adjusted the strap on her shoulder. Sometimes forgiveness required action, even if the emotions weren't cooperating. "Okay, Nigel…that sounds good."

A sparkle filled his green eyes, and the corners of his mouth curved slightly. "All right then."

"I'm headed out for a weekend fishing trip later this afternoon," Lucy said. "So I'll be hard to reach, but you can leave a message on my machine if you find out anything."

Nigel picked his coffee cup off the file cabinet. "I'll keep Eli in the loop as much as I can."

Lucy walked with a lighter step as she made her way back to her van. Would Nigel do what he said? She had no way of knowing. She did know that it had felt good to voice her apology and to hear Nigel's willingness to try to make things right. Officer Peterson was just one cop out of the three that had been on the force four years ago, but it was a start.

When she arrived at the duplex, Lucy shaded her eyes and stared at Eli's closed door. Was Eli avoiding her or was he just busy with work like Nigel had said? Over the past two days, she had heard him come and go. The one time she'd caught him on his way out the door, he had seemed distracted. He was pretty short on conversation. Yet he was coming home in the middle of the day as if to check on her.

She walked around to the back of her van, opened the back door and scanned the gear she had put together for the Memorial Day weekend fishing trip. Lucy took in a deep breath. Eli's actions didn't make any sense—trying to figure him out was making her head hurt.

She scanned the equipment she had packed. Heather would be going with her to help, along with ten paying clients. She had hoped for a few more clients to sign up. These months before the weather was consistently warm could be kind of lean financially.

Being out on the river would be a good way to get her mind off of everything that had happened, and it would help her stop thinking about Eli. She flipped open the first-aid kit, running through a checklist in her head to see what she needed to replenish.

She had to let thoughts of Eli go. No harm, no foul. She and Eli hadn't even been on an official date. Maybe she had just been reading him wrong, assuming he had feelings for her. She slipped the earbuds of her iPod into her ears and turned the music to full blast.

Lucy shook the fishing poles in their racks to make sure they were secure. Most of the people would be bringing their own gear and sleeping bags, but it never hurt to be prepared.

She closed her eyes and stood back, taking in a powerful song chorus. As the music moved toward a climax, the words reminded her that there was no fear for those who loved God. She had heard that truth a hundred times, but had she ever really lived it? She opened her eyes and stared again at all the equipment she had packed in the van. It was one thing to be prepared, and it was another thing to think that all this stuff would prevent bad things from happening.

Lucy shook her head, pulled some of the extra equipment out of the van and tossed it on the ground. She stopped for a moment, closing her eyes again, to listen to the song that played in her ears.

A shadow crossed her path as if a blanket had been thrown on her. She looked up, expecting to see a bird or an airplane. Except for a few drifting clouds, the blue sky was empty.

She sensed someone was standing behind her. Eli? She turned. Her spirit deflated when she saw that it was Greg Jackson. Her music had been so loud, she hadn't heard his car pull up.

She slipped the earbuds out.

"I saw Heather in town a while ago." Greg lifted the straw cowboy hat he was wearing off his head and bent the brim. "She said you were taking some people on an overnight fishing trip."

"Yes, we're going to camp Friday and Saturday night."

"I want to go with you." He must have detected her hesitation because he added, "As a paying client. I'd like to work on my fishing skills."

"Sure, Greg, I've got room."

"I can give you a check right now." There was something pained and desperate in his expression. "Can I ride out with you? My car is not really made for driving up in the mountains."

"What do you have in the way of gear?" She suspected this was a last-minute decision on Greg's part. "I supply the tents if needed, and I can rustle up almost anything else, too."

"I always have my fly rod with me." He chuckled. "I drive so much. Every once in a while I see a beautiful river and just have to stop and fish it."

Greg had never mentioned before that he liked to fish. Given that she fished for a living, it ought to have come up in conversation. She was touched that he was trying to make some kind of connection with her. In her effort to keep her word to Heather, she had probably sent Greg some really ambiguous signals. She would tread lightly around his feelings, but if he was coming with her on this trip, she needed to make sure they were on the same page with their relationship. "Greg, I've decided not to do the online dating thing anymore."

His face brightened as he leaned toward her. "Oh, really. Have you met someone special?"

She had met someone special, but he wasn't around anymore. Greg had totally misunderstood her comment. "You are more than welcome to come on this trip. I enjoy your company, but I really think we should just be friends."

Greg's mouth drooped. "Okay." The tone of his voice implied that he didn't quite believe her. "I don't have a sleeping bag with me."

"Just so we understand each other. We're just friends, right?"

He nodded.

"Good then, load up whatever you have with you. I am sure I can find another sleeping bag. I'll just go inside and grab one." She picked up the things she'd pulled out of the van and darted up the stairs without waiting for a reaction from him. She hadn't wanted to hurt him, but it had felt good to clarify their relationship.

Lucy turned the knob on her door and left it open while she darted up to her loft, where she kept extra camping and fishing supplies. She rifled through several cupboards before she found a sleeping bag appropriate for the season and the right size for a tall man like Greg.

She scampered down the stairs. Greg stood in the doorway.

"You find one?" His voice had taken on a low, husky quality.

She held up the bag. "We should get going. Memorial Day weekend is a great time to be out on the river."

Greg still didn't budge. He was tall enough that he blocked out most of the light streaming through the open door.

As he moved toward her, his footsteps echoed on the wooden floor. "I'm looking forward to being with you." His Adam's apple moved up and down. He lifted his chin. His eyes narrowed. Something about his expression, maybe it was the hardness of his features and the slant of his eyebrows, struck her as unpleasant and brooding.

Lucy took a step back. This house reminded her too much of the assault that had just happened. Maybe that was why her heart was racing.

Lucy handed Greg the sleeping bag. "Load up whatever you have and get in the van."

She did a quick walk through her house, making sure the window, now repaired, was latched. She clicked the dead bolt on the kitchen door. As she locked the front door, a feeling of unease permeated her emotions.

She wiggled the doorknob, double-checking to make sure it was locked. Would her stalker be back to steal something else? Hopefully, Eli would be around more so he could keep an eye on things. She hadn't had a chance to tell him about her trip.

She bounded down the stairs with one backward glance at Eli's closed door. Lucy slipped into the driver's side of the van and clicked on her seat belt. Even as she offered Greg a faint smile, a heaviness she recognized as heartache settled on her. She had begun to open her heart to Eli and that was where it would end.

"You have kind of a faraway look in your eyes." Greg leaned toward her.

Lucy shifted into Reverse and turned the car around. "It's nothing…just thinking." *About things that might have been.*

"Catching some trout should be fun," Greg offered.

Greg's unwavering gaze made her wiggle in her seat as she turned out onto the gravel road and headed toward the river.

"Yes, we should be able to catch something." She needed to get away from this house and out on the water, where she always found peace and the world made sense.

"I'm looking forward to this drive with you." Greg's voice slipped into a hoarse whisper.

A sense of uneasiness rose up in Eli as he pulled into the gravel drive by the duplex and recognized Greg Jackson's car. He'd just gotten word from Officer Smith that Greg Jackson had canceled his date with her tonight. What was Jackson up to?

Eli squeezed the steering wheel a little tighter. Lucy's van was gone.

He got out of his car, grabbed his briefcase and headed toward Lucy's door. Even as he knocked and called her name, he knew it was futile to hope that she was home safe. She and Greg had gone somewhere in her vehicle. He needed to find out where…and quickly.

He traversed the distance to his own side of the house and unlocked his door. He said a prayer for Lucy's safety as his door swung open. Lucy had a cell phone, but he had no idea what the number was. Mentally, he kicked himself for not thinking to ask for it. She had been on his mind in other ways.

When he was home working, he was always aware if she came and went. Every noise she made seemed to be on a higher volume than the rest of the world. Her footsteps on the floorboards of the porch and the sound of her vehicle starting up always caught his attention. He was tuned in to her as if some invisible cord tied them together.

Keeping his emotional distance from her was the hardest thing he had ever done.

He placed his briefcase on the table by the window. He could probably get her number from one of her friends. He hadn't ever been told Heather's last name, but Nelson might know where Lucy was.

Eli rooted through a cupboard to find the phone book he'd gotten the day before. Fear pulsed in his veins as he flipped it open to find Nelson's number. He'd done everything he could to make sure she was okay. He had been coming home for lunch to check on her. On the days he had to do surveillance out of town, he'd requested a patrol car go out in this direction. Realistically, he couldn't keep an eye on her 24/7. Still, knowing that she was alone with Jackson felt like a blunder on his part.

His finger trailed down the list of phone numbers. It had to be here. He exhaled when his finger landed on Thane, Nelson. Eli dialed the number and paced through his living room. He stood at the window, staring at the pine trees and cottonwoods that surrounded Lucy's property.

Nelson picked up on the fourth ring.

"Nelson, it's Eli. Lucy's..." What was he to her? "Lucy's renter."

"Yeah."

"Listen, I just got home, and a strange car is in Lucy's drive. There's no sign of Lucy, but her car is gone. I don't suppose you know where she might be."

"Is she okay?"

He didn't want to trigger any alarm bells or give away too much by identifying Greg Jackson by name. "I'm just concerned about this car and Lucy being gone."

There was a pause on the other end of the line as if Nelson were formulating an answer or deciding if he should answer at all. "Lucy didn't say anything to you about where she would be?"

It was understandable that he wanted to protect Lucy's privacy. "She's had those two break-ins. Guess I am just kind of worried."

"Oh, right." He relented. "She usually takes clients for an extended fishing trip on Memorial Day weekend."

"Are you going with her?"

"I'm a teacher, remember. I have some work-shops I have to attend out of town. I think Heather said something about going with her."

"Do you know where they went?"

"You don't think somebody has…taken…Lucy."

"No, there is nothing to indicate that. But given the break-ins, it makes sense to check on her. It kind of comes with my job description. Do you know her cell number?"

Nelson gave him the number and then added, "A lot of times she doesn't take it with her. A ringing cell phone messes with the serenity of the weekend. The signal drops out a lot once you get up in the mountains, so it's not of much use, safety-wise."

"Do you know where she was planning on camping?"

"There are a hundred campgrounds she could pick. I know she favors the Beartrap campgrounds by the lake. There is a fishing supply place out that way where Lucy usually fuels up. The owners know her."

"That's enough to go on, thanks."

Eli hung up and grabbed his coat. Before he started his car, he tried Lucy's cell phone. No answer. It had been worth a try.

He struggled to stay under the speed limit as he drove toward the main road. He stopped at the first gas station he saw and got directions to the Beartrap store. Eli barely noticed a landscape of rocks and evergreens clipping by as he sped along the mountain road. To keep his mind from shifting into hyper-worry mode, he prayed.

A psalm floated into his head. "I lift my eyes up to the mountains. Where does my help come from? My help comes from the Lord, the maker of heaven and earth." He glanced up at the high mountain that the curving road had been cut through.

He couldn't control outcomes; he couldn't protect everyone all the time, but whatever the circumstances, God would be there for him.

A sign indicated that the turnoff for the Beartrap campgrounds was a mile away. Eli slowed the car and hit his turn signal. The store was not hard to spot. With the exception of a few cabins off in the distance, it was the only structure around. The dusty sign outside advertised that they sold gas, bait and groceries. RV hookups were also available. Two struggling cottonwoods stood on either side of the low-roofed building.

Eli parked his car off to one side. Four motor homes along with several tents were parked behind the store. The river had slipped in and out of view while he was driving. Now he could hear the distant roar of rushing water but not see it.

He raced into the store, where a teenager with

pink hair and a nose ring stood behind the counter. The rich brown of her skin suggested she spent more time outside than in the dim store.

"I am wondering if a woman with long, dark hair came in here earlier. She's a fly fishing guide, and she is taking a bunch of people to the lake."

"You're talking about Lucy Kimbol."

Hope fluttered through him as he stepped around a stack of boxes. "Yes, do you know where she is camping?"

"She reserved several spots up by Madison Point. People who said they were with her have gone through here today, but I haven't seen Lucy yet."

He swallowed to produce some moisture in his mouth. He didn't know anything for sure yet. No need to panic. "Could you have missed her? Or maybe she didn't stop here this time."

The girl shook her head. "I've been behind this counter since ten o'clock. And even if people don't stop, I see them go by. Lucy's van is pretty distinctive. She must have been delayed."

His shoulders slumped. This meant she might be driving around with Greg Jackson...or worse.

The myriad metal bracelets on the teenager's wrist jingled when she lifted her arm and grabbed a map from a rack. "I can give you directions to the camp if you like. I'm sure she'll show up sooner or later."

Eli massaged his chest where it felt tight. "I guess that is the best option."

The young woman gave directions that included things like turning right at the rock with the tree growing out of it. When she finished, she said, "You can keep the map, no charge."

He thanked her and headed out the door. Maybe Lucy had just stopped somewhere for supplies or had a flat tire. He shouldn't think worst-case scenario.

Eli hopped in his car and headed up the road until he found the marked turnoff the teenager had told him about. The road followed the river. He half expected and hoped that he would see Lucy's van before he even got to the camp.

He came to a crossroads and took a right. Several cars, none of them Lucy's van, came into view. The road ended where the land sloped gently down. The silver shimmer of a lake was visible through the trees. When he got out of his car, Eli saw several tents set up in a circle around a fire pit.

He counted five people milling around the camp and three lined up against the edge of the lake, fishing. He trotted down the hill toward the camp.

An older woman in a lime-green T-shirt with large flowers on it noticed him. "Are you one of Lucy's clients? We've all just been getting acquainted and waiting for her."

"She's not here yet?"

The woman shook her head. "I'm sure she'll be along. I'm Betty Daniels, by the way. Lucy taught me how to fly fish just last year." Betty lifted her chin proudly. "I hold the record for being her oldest client."

Eli glanced around the camp. There seemed to be an equal number of men and women. He recognized one of Lucy's high school students from the day he'd rented her duplex, a chubby-cheeked teenager named Marnie. The girl waved at Eli when he made eye contact.

"I hope Lucy gets here soon." The older woman swatted at a mosquito on her arm. "Some of us brought our own tents, but she supplies the others, and she's bringing all the cooking equipment. What did you say your name was?"

"Eli Hawkins."

"Why don't you go down to the lake and enjoy the beauty of God's creation. Lucy will be along anytime now."

He hoped that was true. Maybe he should retrace his steps back into town to see if he could find her. Doing nothing never felt right to him, but he could at least wait a few minutes. Eli tromped down to the edge of the lake. He sat on a flat stump and listened to the sound of the water lapping against the shore while he tapped his foot on the soft dirt. Ten minutes passed. Where was she?

Though there was no dock, several boats and a canoe were arranged upside down not far from the water's edge, along with some float tubes. Lucy must have hauled those up earlier. Behind him, he could hear the sound of people laughing and chatting.

The sky was a clear blue now, but it would start to get dark in a couple of hours. The sun slipped a little lower on the horizon. Eli allowed the soothing murmur of the water to relax him. The memory of the afternoon he and Lucy had spent on the river flashed through his mind.

A shout rose up from the camp and Eli turned. Lucy's van came into view at the top of the hill. Doors slammed, and he saw Heather's blond ponytail and then Greg Jackson gripping a fishing pole. The hat Jackson wore covered his face, but Eli recognized the hunch in his shoulders. Lucy appeared a moment later from the back of the van, holding a cooler.

Eli let out a sigh of relief.

He remained on the edge of camp while the others circled around Lucy. She was wearing a hot pink shirt that made her stand out from the group. Several people ran up to the van and pulled out supplies. With Greg here, it made sense to hang around for as long as he could.

He stalked up the hill and asked a middle-aged man who stood by the van if there was anything he could take down to the camp. The man stacked several tents in storage bags in Eli's arms.

"I'm sure we'll be needing these," said the man.

The hard metal of the tent poles pressed against Eli's forearm through the nylon fabric. He made his way down the hill and sought out Lucy. Her pink shirt was easy enough to spot. Her back was turned toward him as she kneeled beside an open cooler.

"Where should I put these?"

She jerked around and rose to her feet. Her distressed expression chilled him.

The last thing I wanted to do was cause you pain, Lucy.

"What are you doing here?" She took a step back.

"I came for some fishing lessons from a great teacher."

His compliment did nothing to diminish the

coolness in her eyes. Lucy pulled a package of hot dogs out of the ice chest. "You need to go."

"Look, I know I have been making myself scarce." Even when she was upset with him, he relished being close to her.

Heather came up behind Lucy. "Hey, Eli. I didn't know you were coming this weekend."

"He's not staying," Lucy said flatly.

"He's not?" Heather cut a glance toward Lucy and then looked at Eli. "Oh, well, at least join us for dinner." She took the package of hot dogs. "We should be eating in about twenty minutes."

Lucy turned away and stalked down toward the lake. She lifted her hand to her face, obviously wiping her eyes. Eli stepped toward her, but Heather caught him.

"Give her a moment. I don't know what's happened between you two, but maybe you can get things smoothed out over dinner."

"That's all right." He could watch out for her without having to talk to her. Greg probably wouldn't try anything with all these people around. He punched his fist against the palm of his right hand. Still, it bothered him that she was hurting.

During the meal, Lucy kept her distance, then disappeared altogether. Eli visited with the other clients, looking for any excuse to stay longer.

While he talked to Betty, he scanned the campground. His heart lurched. Lucy stood at the shore with Greg, pushing a canoe into the water.

"What is Lucy doing?" He watched as Greg wandered back up the hill.

Betty crossed her arms. "Some of the clients paid extra for individual instruction. Lucy is probably taking that fellow out on the water. The rest of us are thinking about a sing-along. We've got a couple of guitar players among us. Want to join?"

"I need to take care of something first." Eli strode down to where Lucy was loading gear into the canoe.

"Haven't you left yet?" she asked. She clicked herself into her life jacket.

"I don't think it is a good idea for you to go out on the water alone with that man." He labored to keep his voice calm, to not reveal the hurricane of anxiety brewing inside.

Greg was already on his way back down the hill.

Lucy straightened her back. "He is a client and a friend. He paid for private instruction, and I am taking him out on the lake. You have to stop this…behavior, Eli. It's crazy."

He searched her eyes, desperate to keep her safe on shore. "Please, don't go."

"You can't tell me what to do." Her reprimand

was soft, and he could discern the distress beneath her words. Pain he had caused. Nothing he could say would stop her.

Greg yelled across the camp, holding his fly rod. "I'm ready to go."

Eli stepped away. "Be careful, Lucy."

Lucy and Greg pushed the canoe off the shore and jumped in. As they drifted, Lucy mimed a casting motion while Greg watched her and dragged the paddle through the water.

Maybe he could still keep an eye on her. He was a strong swimmer. If he heard sounds of a struggle, he could jump in the water. Someone had already taken the other boats, but he'd seen the extra fishing rods and waders that Lucy had laid out for anyone to grab.

His shoulders tensed when Lucy's boat slipped behind a peninsula populated with trees.

He worked his way quickly down the shoreline, scanning the water for signs of Lucy's canoe. This part of the lake was narrow enough that he could see the other side of the shore, where several fishermen were visible. Four other boats drifted on the water, as well. Lucy's boat was not overly distinctive, but he recognized her pink shirt. He stepped into the water.

He cast several times. At this distance, Lucy

probably wouldn't even be able to discern that it was him on the shore.

He heard the swishing noise of someone moving through water behind him.

"Mind if you have some company?" Betty smiled and squared her shoulders. "Couldn't quite put the sing-along together, so I decided to get in some practice."

He still had a clear view of the boat, but it was drifting farther away. "I'm just working my way down the river."

Betty drew back her rod. "Getting any hits?"

He squinted. Lucy's pink shirt had become a dot. "No, not really."

"It helps if you actually put your line in the water." Betty drew back her own fly rod and cast. "'Course, you are probably distracted keeping an eye on Lucy while she is with that other guy."

"No, that's not why I'm…um." Betty thought he was watching Lucy because he was jealous of Greg. Was that the impression he was giving?

"You don't need to worry about that guy in the boat with her. You can tell she doesn't like him." Betty reeled in her line. "Nope, I would say the field is wide-open for you."

"I rent half of a duplex from her. We're just friends." He didn't sound convincing even to himself. Even if there could be nothing romantic between them, he cared deeply for Lucy. More so than he had about any other woman.

Betty laughed. "I watched the two of you back at camp. Only people who like each other fight like that. I saw how you changed when her van showed up. I don't know what is stopping the two of you, but I'm sure you can work through it."

Eli sighed. "I wish it were that easy."

"Love is always that easy." The line clicked on Betty's reel. "Just move whatever is standing in the way out of the way."

He scanned the lake, panic rising in his chest. No sign of Lucy's boat. This lake was huge. There were a dozen eddies she could have slipped into. If he watched long enough, she would glide back into view. "I do have feelings for Lucy." Saying the truth out loud intensified the emotion he'd been pushing down.

"I thought so." Betty nodded. "This is a lovely time of night to be out here. Fish are always biting right before the sun goes down." Water whooshed around her as she stepped away from Eli. "Won't catch anything if we keep jabbering."

They cast silently for several minutes as the distance between them increased. Waves lapped against his waders, and the sky turned from blue to gray. Over and over, he scanned the lake in the waning light. Maybe there was enough traffic on the water to prevent Greg from trying anything.

He saw a flash of pink. He had worked his way to a wider part of the lake; the opposite shore was no longer visible.

As the sun slipped behind the horizon, Betty waved at him. She was far enough away that he couldn't hear her even if she shouted. The older woman worked her way to shore and disappeared into the trees.

Slowly the population on the river diminished as fishermen returned to their camps to cook their catch or, more likely, the beans and burgers they had brought with them.

Eli stepped as far into the water as he could in order to get a maximum view of the lake. Even though there were fewer boats, none of them were Lucy's.

He'd lost her.

ELEVEN

Tension pinched the muscles in Lucy's neck. The farther they got away from the camp, the more agitated Greg grew. He cursed when his line caught on something in the water. After they got his line free, Lucy made a suggestion about holding the rod at a different angle.

He tossed his rod into the boat. "I don't want to fish." He crossed his arms and glowered.

"Sorry, I didn't mean to sound bossy."

Eli's words of caution floated back into her head. Why had he been so determined not to let her go out on the water with Greg? As their boat had edged away from the shore, Eli had stood on the beach, watching them. At the time, his actions had confirmed her fear that, despite his kindness, Eli was controlling.

Now as she and Greg drifted farther out, she wondered if Eli's cautions hadn't been valid all along. When Eli had shown up, all she had wanted to do was get away from him and the strong emotions his presence evoked. His hot-cold behavior toward her was too much to take.

Greg stared at the water. Lucy paddled the canoe into a quiet spot where they were likely to catch something.

"Tell you what. I'll cast for a while." She picked up her rod. "You just enjoy the quiet."

Greg unfolded his arms and rubbed them on his thighs. "So what is between you and that Hawkins guy anyway?"

Was that what his pouting was about? "Nothing. We're friends, that's all." Even as she said it, she knew it wasn't true. She wasn't about to get into a relationship with someone whose signals were so inconsistent, but she had to be honest about how much she cared about him.

"You're friends with everyone, every guy." His tone held an undercurrent of irritation.

On the ride up, the thought of having to be alone in the van with Greg was more than she wanted to handle. He kept pressing the conversation toward the personal, as if he hadn't heard that she was only interested in him as a friend. She'd taken a detour and picked up Heather, despite having made plans to meet at the lake, so the conversation would remain light.

"Heather keeps telling me I turn every guy into a friend." She laughed. "Actually, it's what everyone keeps saying."

Her comment seemed to break the tension. Greg chortled and picked up his fly rod. They cast for some time. Greg offered to paddle, and Lucy indicated a place she thought the fish might be biting.

The blue sky of midday faded into a shroud of gray. The gentle plopping sound of the fish rising to the water's surface to feed in the evening increased. Lucy attached a different fly to her tippet. Thinking about Eli, trying to make sense out of everything he had done, made her head hurt. He was a hard man to figure out.

"Lots of fish out here. I don't know why nothing's taking the fly." Greg's words broke through the tumult of her thoughts.

She angled around in the boat, assessing where they were in the fading light. She'd been so lost in thought, she hadn't been paying attention to where Greg was paddling. She'd been out on this lake a thousand times. All she needed was a familiar landmark to know where she was.

"It's almost dark, Greg. We really should be headed back."

She scanned the shoreline, looking for a grove of trees or an outcropping of rock that was distinct.

They were in the wide part of the lake; only one shoreline was visible, and it was distant and dark.

"Is everything okay?" he asked.

She pulled her compass out of one of her pockets. "We're fine, I just need to get a stronger sense of where we are." Lucy held the compass closer to her face, trying to decipher the numbers and letters.

"Lucy, I didn't sign up for your clinic and ask you out here so I could improve my casting technique."

Still gripping the compass, Lucy looked at Greg. His expression wasn't readable in this light, but his tone had warmed.

"What do you mean?" She had a feeling where this was going.

He cleared his throat. "I know that you said you just wanted to be friends."

She couldn't see her compass. She slipped out of her life jacket so she could dig deeper into her vest to find her flashlight. "We can talk about this later, Greg. Right now, we need to focus on getting back to camp."

"I don't want to talk about it later." Greg readjusted himself on the seat with such energy that it shook the canoe.

Lucy dug through her pockets. She zipped and unzipped. She always had her flashlight with her.

It had to be here somewhere. Her stomach tensed in anticipation of what she was pretty sure Greg was going to say.

"I've been wanting to say this for some time, but you always set things up so we are never alone."

Where was that flashlight? Lucy struggled to keep her voice calm. "Greg, I thought you understood that we were just friends." Now she was mad at herself for being in such a hurry to get away from Eli that she hadn't thought about the consequences of being alone with Greg. She had seen this coming when they were in the van, but Eli showing up had thrown clear thinking out the window.

"Not every man in your life wants to just be your best buddy. When are you going to see that?" Greg shouted, standing halfway up in the canoe and then plopping back down with force.

Water sloshed against the side of the boat. She gripped the rim. "Careful, canoes aren't like boats—they tip easily."

Leaning closer to her, he grabbed her hands. "I have stopped dating all the other women I was paired up with. It's you, Lucy. You're the one for me. I've been praying about it."

"Greg, you are a nice guy, but—"

He stood up, looming over her. "God told me you were the one." The boat rocked.

"Greg, please sit down." She raised her voice. He didn't comply. She spoke in a monotone, enunciating every word. "I think you are projecting things onto God because it's what you want."

"I've been patient. I've been nice." He lunged toward her, and she fell backward.

The boat tipped dangerously to one side. He reached for her, and she scrambled to get away from him. Water cascaded into the boat.

"Greg, please sit down."

Greg shot up onto his feet, unsteady as the boat rocked. "When, Lucy, when are you going to see how much I like you?" He wobbled.

He reached for her, yanking her to her feet. "Please, stop," she begged.

The canoe angled dangerously to one side. Greg stumbled, grabbing Lucy to steady himself. Instead, he pulled her into the water with him. The lake engulfed her. She thrashed around, unable to orient in the depths of the cold water.

Something anchored her in place, a weight on her shoulder, like hands holding her down. Lucy kicked her legs, trying to break free, but the weight on her shoulder made it impossible to move.

She needed to breathe. She flailed her arms, then angled downward trying to escape the force clamped on her shoulders. The weight lifted. With a final burst of energy, she scissor-kicked her legs and reached upward.

Lucy swam to the surface, breaking through the water into the dim of evening. She gasped. Breath wheezed through her nose.

She could make out the fuzzy silhouette of the shore. She waited for her eyes to adjust. Slowly the outline of the boat came into view. A soaking wet Greg crawled into the canoe.

"Over here." She swam toward it, her strokes sluggish and uneven. When she stopped to see how close she was, Greg was paddling the boat...away from her. She shouted one more time. The stroke of the paddle stuttered and then he seemed to glide across the water even faster. Stunned, she treaded water as he disappeared around a bend. Had he left her here to drown? She wondered, too, if it hadn't been his hands holding her under.

Lucy turned a slow circle in the lake. Lakes were warmer than rivers, but the cold could be a factor if she stayed in the water too long.

Though distant, the shoreline was visible. It was on the opposite side of the lake from where camp was, but it was dry land. There were campers all around the lake. She'd likely find help.

Lucy shivered. Her arms cut through the water.

She focused on the shoreline, careful to pace herself, so she didn't run out of energy.

She stopped to tread water and catch her breath. Her muscles were heavy, on fire with pain. Water lapped around her.

Her calf muscles contracted. The chill of the water had soaked through to her muscles. Her vest with all its filled pockets was weighing her down. Much as she regretted the loss, she was going to have to let it go. Lucy slipped free of the vest and flipped over on her back. With the night sky as her canopy, she backstroked through the water.

A few stars had already come out. With renewed vigor, she turned over on her stomach and stroked toward the shore. The outlines and shadows of the forest grew closer.

Lucy swam the final yards to shallow water. She didn't have an ounce of energy left. Her feet brushed over the rocky bottom of the lake. She pulled herself the rest of the way out of the water, collapsing on the muddy shore. Her lungs felt as if they'd been scraped with a utility knife, and her arms and legs burned from exertion.

She pressed her face against the earth, waiting to get her breathing under control. Every part of her felt heavy, numb and cold. Her head seemed as if it was stuffed full of marbles. She closed her eyes, listening to her own raspy, rapid breathing, waiting for it to slow down.

She rolled over on her back and stared at the night sky. Stars twinkled back at her. Could Eli have been right about Greg? Had he tried to hold her under water? She closed her eyes. Eli had tried to warn her from the beginning. She'd been too stubborn to listen at first and then, tonight, too blinded by hurt.

She sat up, pulling her knees to her chest. The night was chilly, but not freezing. Her wet clothes clung to her body. First things first—she needed to get warm and dry. She placed a palm on her shoulder expecting to feel the pocket of her vest. Her heart sank. The waterproof matches were in the vest she had peeled off in the water.

Lucy shivered and stared up at the dark sky.

"Are you sure you'll be all right going alone?" Heather asked as she opened the back of Lucy's van. "They always say it's better to work in pairs."

Eli loaded his pack with everything he thought he might need for a night search. He ignored the panic that had invaded his thoughts ever since Lucy had slipped out of view in the boat. He stuffed a flashlight in his pack. "At this point, I think we need to divide our efforts. If I'm not back in camp by daylight, you can send a search party out for me."

Heather nodded. "I'm going to take the road around the lake one more time to see if I can spot their boat, and then I'll head back to camp to wait for news from the others."

Eli clamped a supportive hand on Heather's shoulder. "We'll find them." It wasn't the thought of Lucy being out in the elements or the possibility that something had gone wrong with the boat that worried him. Lucy was experienced enough to deal with the wilderness. The problem was that she was with Greg Jackson.

When it had grown dark and Lucy and Greg hadn't shown up, two people from the camp had gone down the mountain to notify the police and search and rescue. Campers all along the shoreline had taken their boats out to search the water. Others had gone out to check the trails.

After saying goodbye to Heather, Eli turned onto the trail. The waxing gibbous moon provided some light as he trudged on the hard ground. He'd kept thoughts of Lucy and what might have happened to her at bay by focusing on organizing the search. Now that he was alone, hundreds of crime-scene pictures flashed through his head.

If something happened to Lucy, he would never

forgive himself. Greg had been the last person she'd been seen with. Certainly he wouldn't try anything.

That rationality did nothing to make him less anxious. The forest grew thicker, blocking out the moon. Eli switched on his flashlight.

Lucy had become such an important part of his life. She mattered to him more than any woman he'd known. His throat tightened. What would he do without her?

He couldn't keep his distance. He didn't want to. He loved her.

The trail beneath his feet had gotten narrower until it had disappeared all together. Eli took a few steps through the dense forest, hoping to find the trail again. His flashlight flickered. Great, the batteries were going dead.

As he banged the flashlight against his palm to get it to work, he refused to believe that anything had happened to her. He would find her.

Lucy's teeth chattered as she crossed her arms over her body. She had been walking for close to an hour. She'd stayed close to the lake, yet she hadn't come across a single camper.

The night sounds of the forest, branches creaking and waves lapping against the shore, surrounded her. The scent of pine and mountain cleanness hung in the air. From the time Grandpa had first taken her backpacking, the forest had never been a scary place. Being this close to God's creation comforted her even now, though she was cold and tired.

With her strength renewed, she vowed to get home and apologize to Eli. He had been right about Greg.

Lucy stepped into a clearing.

The glow from lanterns and fires should make it easy to find campers. The people from her party must have been alarmed by now. Greg's behavior had been so strange. Would he go back to camp? She doubted it. What kind of believable story could he tell about her whereabouts?

A branch cracked. Lucy's breath caught. She glanced around, looking for something to use as a weapon. A deer emerged from the trees, followed by a second doe. They sauntered across the clearing. Lucy stood still, not wanting to alarm them or destroy the sacredness of the moment. The deer came down to the water and dipped its head to drink. Lucy held her breath and willed herself to be a statue. Moonlight washed over them. Their heads shot up. White tails flickered.

They suddenly bolted back into the trees,

opposite the direction they had come from. Something had scared them. Every ambient sound fell away as she focused on the forest. A breaking branch crackled.

Lucy tensed. A shadow emerged from the trees. Could be a man. Could be an animal. Something was definitely over there. It was too far to run to the trees where the deer had fled. She edged toward the water.

The shadow separated, and she saw that it was a man. Greg maybe? Had he come looking for her to finish the job he had started on the lake?

She eased into a crouch by the water, hoping to blend into her surroundings. Her heart hammered. Kneeling made her keenly aware of how much her tired muscles ached.

The man, still shrouded in shadow, moved across the clearing, stopped, cupped his hands over his mouth and yelled, "Lucy!"

She knew that voice. "Eli." She sprang to her feet, closing the distance between them.

Eli enveloped her, wrapping his arms around her, repeating her name over and over. "I am so glad to see you." He stroked her hair. "We were looking for you everywhere."

She rested her face against his chest. "Eli, you were right...about Greg."

"Lucy, I…" He kissed the top of her head. "When I thought something…"

She pulled back and looked up at him. Something about him had changed. The intensity of his gaze drew her in.

His fingertips brushed her temple and trailed down her cheek. He leaned toward her and pressed his lips against hers. She touched the roughness of his face as he deepened the kiss. Her skin tingled. His hand rested on her back, pulling her even closer.

He released her from the kiss. His smile faded. "I had some time to think about you, about us." He rested his fingers beneath her jaw, lifting her chin slightly. "I know you fear losing people you love. Don't let that fear control you. I'm here. You don't have to be afraid anymore. I am not going anywhere."

"I want that to be true." Lucy closed her eyes, and he kissed each lid.

"Almost losing you made me realize what I have to do," he whispered. He nestled his face against her neck. His lips grazed her skin.

She melted against him. This was where she had longed to be, safe in Eli's arms. Why had she fought his kindness, his need to protect her, for so long? Was fear really ruling her choices?

He pulled free, still resting his palm on her

back. He touched her wet hair with his other hand. "We need to build a fire and get you dry and warm. I have something to tell you." He pulled his jacket off and draped it over her shoulders.

"A fire? I ditched my vest in the lake because it was weighing me down. My matches were in there."

He placed a warm finger on her lips. He reached into the pocket of the jacket he had just given her and pulled out a tiny box. "Waterproof matches. I grabbed them out of your van."

He slipped his hand in hers and guided her across the clearing toward a flat rock. "You sit here. I'll get some wood together."

"I can help."

"No, Lucy." He tucked a strand of hair behind her ear, tracing the outline of her ear with his finger. "You have been through so much. You don't have to do everything."

"Okay." Lucy sat down on a large rock. The warmth of Eli's touch lingered on her skin. Her limbs, which a few minutes before had felt heavy from exertion, now were light like helium.

Eli sauntered toward the forest, leaning over to gather logs and twigs. She was shivering by the time he got back with wood. He stacked the sticks into a teepee shape and placed the kindling inside the structure.

"After we get you warmed up, we'll hike out," he said.

"How far are we from camp?"

"Heather dropped me off at the trailhead. I walked for about an hour." With the fire going, he sat on the rock beside her. Eli poked at the burning logs with a stick.

Lucy held her hands out closer to the fire. Eli's leg pressed against hers. She breathed in his clean soap smell. Explanations could come later. For now, she just wanted to savor this moment. Eli had promised not to leave her and that was all that mattered.

Feeling even more protective of Lucy, Eli wrapped an arm around her shoulder. Betty's advice echoed through his head. Love was easy, you just needed to move whatever was in the way out of the way. What was in the way was this investigation. "There is a reason why I was concerned about you being with Greg."

"I even had an inkling about him when I was driving up here." Lucy crossed her arms over her chest and stared at the fire. "I wasn't thinking straight. I wanted to get away from you. My emotions were so mixed up."

"I understand. I know I sent you really mixed

signals." His pulse rate increased. Would telling her the truth drive them apart? The kiss had melted his feet in his shoes. He'd wanted to do that for a long time. He turned his head and kissed her cheek, basking in the warmth of being so close to her.

She tugged the coat up around her shoulders. "I think Greg tried to drown me." She shuddered, and he squeezed her tighter. "What if he was the one who was in my place those two times?"

He still viewed the robberies as a separate crime. Lucy's assumption was logical since she didn't know anything about the investigation.

Eli cleared his throat. He had done everything he could, and Lucy was safe. He had to let go of feeling like he hadn't done enough to protect her. "What makes you say he tried to hurt you?"

"He pulled us both out of the boat...and I...I thought he held me under water."

He rubbed her arm. "But you're not sure?"

"It all happened so fast. I think falling in the water was an accident, but then..." She stiffened. "Did they find Greg?"

"No. He never came back to the camp. We have a ton of people looking for both of you all around the lake."

"He took off in the boat. I know he heard me shouting. Why did he leave me there?"

Greg's behavior did sound suspicious. "You're still shivering. Why don't we sit a little closer?"

She slipped off the rock and used it as a backrest. He tossed another log onto the blazing fire and sat down beside her.

After a moment, she rested her head against him. Her breathing deepened as she fell asleep. He held her, watching the flames in the fire and enjoying her closeness.

She stirred. He wrapped an arm around her, and she nestled closer. He touched her soft hair.

Eli stared out into the darkness and listened to the soft rhythm of Lucy's breathing. She had stopped shivering. He'd missed his opportunity to tell her about the investigation. Maybe it was better this way. He'd clear it with the chief first. Lucy needed to know. He was tired of the deception.

He'd have to wake her in a few minutes. He tilted his head to stare at the twinkling stars and prayed for more chances to hold Lucy. There was still so much in the way.

One thing was clear. If Greg had tried to drown Lucy and then left her, they had a reason for bringing him in. Then maybe this investigation would be wrapped up and out of their lives.

Ten minutes later, Lucy opened her eyes and sat up.

"Hey, sleepyhead. Let's go see if we can find some help."

They hiked for hours toward the trailhead in the rose light of predawn until they found a camper who was willing to take them back to their camp. Heather and Betty were the only ones still there when they showed up. Betty greeted them with a hug and returned to taking down tents.

Heather wrapped an arm around her friend. "I'll get the word out that we found you." She squeezed Lucy's shoulder. "You look tired and beat-up. I can wait here to notify the others. Why don't you ride back in with Eli? I'll bring the van in later."

Eli slipped his hand into Lucy's. "Has Greg Jackson been found?"

Heather shook her head. "They found the boat pulled ashore, but no sign of him. Go home and get some rest. Betty and I can do any cleanup that needs to be done."

They drove down the mountain in Eli's car with the sun brimming on the horizon. As they neared the duplex, Eli checked his phone. His signal was back, and he had twelve messages.

Lucy leaned toward him. "Something wrong?"

He paged through the messages as ice froze in his veins. All the calls were from William's cell or the police station. He dialed William's number.

William picked up before the first ring ended. "Where have you been? We've had another murder over in Cragmore."

TWELVE

Eli's stomach churned as he stepped under the crime scene tape. William emerged from a tight circle of people. He handed a framed photo to his partner. Outside, two police cars were parked beside William's car.

"Jessica Mason, age twenty-six." William turned slightly. "Most of the crime scene work is done. When I couldn't get hold of you, I opted to have the body taken in for autopsy. I figured we have to move fast on this."

A chill ran down Eli's back. He stared at the photo of the dark-haired, blue-eyed woman. "This shouldn't have happened on my watch."

"It shouldn't happen on anybody's watch. Don't beat yourself up."

"Thanks for the reminder." Eli glanced around the simply furnished living room. "What about our suspects? Did any of them have contact with our victim?"

"Far as we know, none of the three came near here. We've only done preliminary questioning. Something might turn up later. Is Jackson still unaccounted for?"

Eli nodded. He had already explained the reason he couldn't answer his phone to William. When he had pulled up to Lucy's duplex, Greg's car was still parked there. Lucy had promised she would go to a neighbor's house until Heather showed up with the van.

"Thought you might want to do a walk-through before we go to the morgue." William gestured for Eli to follow him. "The prelim exam suggests it might have been strangulation."

"That fits the M.O. of the other victims." Eli's footsteps seemed to echo in the cold, still house. "Who found her?"

"Paper boy. She's always sitting on her porch with her cup of coffee, waiting for him. She wasn't there this morning."

A hot sear of pain jabbed through Eli. Jessica would never sit on her porch again. "So she could have died last night?"

"We're trying to track down who may have seen her last and find out what she did yesterday." William's voice trailed off. This was hitting them both harder than they wanted to admit.

"We should probably keep the crime scene tape up, just in case we need to go through again in light of what the autopsy reveals." Time of death was paramount. Cragmore wasn't that far from Mountain Springs. If the TOD had been early Friday or before, Jackson could have been here before he headed up the mountain with Lucy.

Eli came into the kitchen, which was painted a fresh shade of yellow. Nothing in the kitchen indicated that someone had started to make coffee or begun a morning routine.

Two clean plates and wineglasses rested in the drying rack, signs of a dinner date.

"I've got an officer working the neighborhood to see if they saw anyone coming or going," William offered.

A calendar with pictures of wildflowers hung on the wall. There were three cat stickers on the Saturday, Sunday and Monday of Memorial Day weekend. He lifted the calendar to June. She'd put a cat sticker on Father's Day, as well. That small detail about Jessica, that she marked all the holidays ahead of time with cute stickers, intensified the ache he felt in his chest.

Eli jerked back. Something about the calendar haunted him. He touched the picture of daisies in a field that represented the month of May.

William patted his shoulder. "Why are you looking at the calendar?"

Eli shook his head. His finger trailed over one of the cat stickers. "She didn't have dates with any of the other three suspects. What about with Jackson?"

"That's just it. Her picture never came up on any of the surveillance. We took her laptop in for evidence."

Eli's throat went dry. "That throws a wrench in it." But Jessica did have dark hair and blue eyes.

"I still think it's the same guy. This is too rural an area to think we are dealing with two killers. Nothing in the media ties the deaths together, so it can't be a copycat."

"I agree. We have to figure out what the link is between her and the others." Eli moved toward the hallway and stepped back out on the porch. The street was quiet. In the distance, children laughed and played. A woman on the other side of the street sauntered by with a dog on a leash. Eli's mind whirred a mile a minute. "Do we know where she worked?"

"The paper boy didn't know. The landlord is absentee. She didn't have any family close by as far as we know. Her mom is flying in to identify the body."

Eli trotted down the stairs with William close behind him. He felt a sense of urgency in his stride as he made his way to the car. Now the clock was ticking. They had to find this guy before his path crossed another dark-haired, blue-eyed woman.

The Mountain Springs police station buzzed with activity, most of which centered around all the information-gathering taking place to catch Jessica's killer. Eli rubbed the stubble that had formed on his face. His eyes were blurry from reading the reports over and over. What was he missing?

Officer Nigel Peterson made his way toward Eli's desk. He ran his fingers through his thinning red hair. "I know you're really focused on the big case, but I promised Lucy I would keep you up to speed on her robberies."

Eli sat up a little straighter. Even though O'Bannon and Spitz hadn't let go of their grudge toward Lucy, Officer Peterson had made a concerted effort at attitude change. "What did you find?"

"I told you about her suspicions concerning her high school coach, George Whitmore."

Eli nodded. The thought of anyone harassing Lucy when she was a vulnerable high school student made his blood boil.

"He has never had any charges against him. But when I talked to some people at the school where he taught after leaving here, they hinted of inappropriate behavior toward the girls he coached." Nigel placed a photograph on Eli's desk. "From the high school yearbook."

Eli stared at the photo of a lean man with dark hair. His grin took up most of his face. "I took fingerprint samples from after Lucy's first robbery, but if he doesn't have a record, he won't be in any databases."

"I can see if I can find a way to get his prints. Maybe he was in the military."

As much as he wanted to resolve Lucy's robberies, he needed to focus on Jessica Mason's murder. "Thank you for doing that, Nigel."

Eli returned to reading the compiled reports for what felt like the hundredth time. He spread the hard copies of the photographs out on his desk. Jessica just looked too much like the others to dismiss her outright, even though she wasn't connected to the dating service.

He tapped a pencil on his desk. If he pulled out the dating service as a factor, what linked the women together besides looks? Maybe Jessica's death was a crime of opportunity.

Eli stroked the stubble on his cheek. He hadn't been home for more than a few hours for the last two days. He had called Lucy at least twice a day. The sound of her voice revived him. The chief had not given him permission to disclose the details of the investigation to Lucy. His gut told him he was close to an arrest. After that, he and Lucy could be together.

Greg Jackson was still unaccounted for. His car had been taken to the impound yard. Authorities had combed the whole area around the lake, and all the local departments in nearby towns were told to notify him right away if they spotted Greg or if an unidentified body was found anywhere.

Eli returned to his notes. Jessica Mason had worked as a manager at a sandwich shop. She had lived in Cragmore for five months and everyone had liked her. Neither coworkers, friends or neighbors said Jessica had ever mentioned being signed up for a dating service. Nothing in her apartment or on her laptop indicated any connection to the online service.

One neighbor had seen a car she hadn't recognized parked Friday night on the block where Jessica lived.

Eli rose to his feet and paced through the station. His stopped at the watercooler, his back to his desk. He filled his cup with water.

William came up behind him. "The officer watching Greg Jackson's place said a taxi just dropped him off at his home. The deputy in Jacob's Corner is picking him up now. Thought you might want to be there for the questioning."

Finally, a break. This could be it. He bent his neck side to side and blinked in an effort to find more energy.

An odd hush permeated the police station. When Eli turned around, Lucy was standing by his desk; a picnic basket rested on the floor beside her. She held one of the victims' photos in her hand. The stiff backs and stares of Officers O'Bannon and Spitz added to the tension of the moment.

The look of devastation on Lucy's face made his knees buckle. He squeezed the paper cup he was holding. "Lucy, what are you doing here?"

She pointed to the picnic basket. "I wanted to surprise you with lunch." Lucy waved the photograph in the air. "What is all this?"

He wasn't going to lie to her. "It's the investigation I was brought in to lead." Eli tossed his paper cup and gathered up the photographs and reports.

"Those women look like me. What is going on?" Her breath caught. "Did Greg Jackson hurt them?"

"I don't know if he did or not. But we are getting close to finding out." He reached out to touch her arm, but she pulled away.

William hovered close by. "We got to go, boss."

Eli held up his hand. "Just a second." He stepped toward Lucy. A punch in the gut would hurt less than the expression on her face. "I wanted to tell you, but we couldn't risk having this guy go underground and start killing again years from now."

"Is that the only reason you spent time with me?" Her eyes glazed. "Because it helped you find your killer?"

"No." His voice broke. What had he done?

"So if you were brought in for the investigation that means you're leaving after it's done. Soon as this guy is caught, you're going back to Spokane, right?"

"That was the original plan." But so much had changed.

"Hawkins, we need to get going," William pressed.

She shook her head. "I trusted you. Was everything you told me a lie?"

"I meant every word I said. Please believe me." He longed to gather her in his arms. "I have to go do this interview. I want to talk later. I can explain."

"I have to go to my brother's murderball tournament later." Her voice took on the wavering tone of a person trying to hold back tears. "You don't have to explain anything."

Eli watched her stalk out of the police station as a sense of overwhelming despair invaded every part of his being.

THIRTEEN

Eli stared at Greg Jackson hunched over a table in the police station. The station was too small to have an interrogation room, so one of the officers had set up a table and chairs in a quiet corner.

He struggled to clear his mind of thoughts about Lucy. He had wanted to tell her that he would quit his job in Spokane in a heartbeat. That while she had started out as a lead in his case, she had become so much more to him. He'd be a small-town cop if it allowed him to be close to her, but the look on her face had rendered him nearly speechless.

Maybe it would be better if he stayed out of her life. The last thing in the world he wanted to do was hurt her, and yet he had managed to do it over and over.

William patted Eli on the back. "Let's get this done, huh?" He held the envelope that contained the photos of the other victims.

Eli stopped at the water fountain and filled a paper cup.

Greg Jackson's face paled as they advanced toward him. Eli placed the cup of water on the table. "Thought you might be thirsty."

"Thank you," Jackson whimpered. He crossed his arms and rested his chin on his chest.

Eli slipped into the chair opposite Jackson while William remained standing. "Do you know why you are here?"

"'Cause you think I tried to hurt Lucy."

Eli had assumed that Jackson would be fixated on Lucy's accident. That line of questioning served as a warm-up to asking him about the other women. He leaned forward, hoping the action would force Jackson to make eye contact. "Did you?"

Greg's glance flickered up, but then he stared at the table. "Not on purpose. It's just that…" He ran a clawlike hand through his hair. "I wanted her to have feelings for me."

"You say you care about her." Eli rested his hands on the table. "Why did you take the canoe and leave her in the lake?"

"I know I have an anger problem. I was afraid of getting out of control." The cup shook in his hand as he took a sip of water. "I knew she was a good swimmer. I thought she would be okay."

Eli shifted in his chair. He could still only see Greg's profile, making it hard to read his facial expression. "Did you try to drown her, hold her under?"

Greg swung around in his chair. "She just made me so upset. I saw how out of control I was, so I left." He licked his lips.

"You tried to drown her," Eli pressed.

Jackson stared at the ceiling. "I might have pushed her down."

"You held her under?"

Greg blinked and then closed his eyes. "Yes, but I stopped. I left."

William moved in closer. The envelope he held crinkled in his hand. "Why didn't you go back to the camp?"

"Because I was ashamed." Greg scooted his chair back and bent his chin toward his chest. "I didn't want to see Lucy. I didn't want to face the others."

William stood behind Eli. "Where did you go?"

"I rowed to shore. I wandered through the forest until I found a camper to take me into town."

"A camper. What was his name?" Eli asked.

For the first time, Greg looked directly at Eli. "Why do you want to know? Lucy did make it to shore okay, didn't she?" Jackson's concern seemed genuine.

"She's fine. What was the name of the camper?"

"He said his name was Joe. I don't remember his last name. I think it started with a *T.* He drove a jeep, and he said he worked as a carpenter in Mountain Springs."

The details of his answer were too specific to be lies. "Why didn't you come back for your car?"

"I didn't want to have to face Lucy, don't you understand?" His fist hit the table with a half-hearted thump. "I was ashamed of the way I acted. I just thought if I could get her alone and talk to her, she would see how much I liked her."

"Where have you been for the last two days?"

"I went to a hotel. I needed to think things through." Greg's breathing had become labored enough for the rise and fall of his chest to be noticeable.

Eli stared at Greg, hoping it might unhinge him. Greg scooted his chair forward and then back again. He was capable of violence, but was he capable of murder? Eli lifted his chin as a signal to William.

William pulled photographs of the victims from the envelope and laid them on the table. "Do you know any of these women?"

Greg studied each photograph. "They all look like Lucy, but not as pretty." He placed a finger on one of the photographs. "I had a date with her. All she did was talk about her ex-husband." He lifted the picture of Jessica Mason. His cheeks turned tomato-red. "This is about the thing that was in the paper, isn't it? The woman who died in Cragmore. You don't think I would ever…" Greg shook his head in disbelief. "I know that it is wrong to get angry at women, but I wouldn't kill anyone."

William's cell phone rang; he stepped away from the table to answer it.

"Where were you on Friday before you met up with Lucy at her house?"

"Now, that is just too much." Greg pushed the chair back and stood up.

"Sit down," Eli soothed. He was well versed on the games that psychotic killers played when questioned. It was entirely possible that Greg had assumed the role of victim to detract from his guilt.

Greg collapsed back into the chair and rested his face in his hands. "I don't want to be like my dad was with my mom." He rocked back and forth.

Jackson's voice was mournful, filled with agony. Yes, killers like the one they were chasing were adept at mask wearing, but something in Eli's gut told him that Greg was sincere.

William snapped his phone shut, walked over to Eli and whispered, "Can I talk to you for a minute?"

Eli stood up and stepped away from Greg. He huddled with William.

William spoke in a hushed whisper. "Got the finals on the autopsy. The M.E. puts the time of death for Jessica somewhere between late Friday afternoon and early Friday night."

Eli turned back around to look at Greg, whose face was buried in his hands. That would be the time when Greg was with Lucy and then the other campers. "If we can locate the camper who gave Greg a ride into town, it would be impossible for him to have been at Jessica's house."

"Let's assume he has an alibi." William nodded. "Are we back to square one?"

Eli thoughts whirled a mile a minute. Something Greg had said floated back into his mind. "Not quite square one."

William tilted his head toward Greg. "What should we do with him?"

"He admits to holding Lucy under water. We can charge him for that. He's guilty of a lot of things, but I don't think murder is one of them. We need to get back to the station."

After giving instructions about Greg to the local officer, Eli and William left the small station and headed to the car. Eli got into the passenger side of the Volkswagen after removing the papers he had stacked there. Talking to Lucy had flustered him so much, he'd brought the picture of George Whitmore with him. He glanced at the picture of Lucy's high school coach. The image of Jessica's calendar on her wall materialized in his mind. His heartbeat quickened. Everything suddenly clicked into place.

William started up his car. "What is it?"

"You tracked down Jessica's employer, right?"

William nodded. "I have her name in my notes."

"You need to find out exactly what Jessica was doing, where she was Friday afternoon. Why don't you go back to the station and get me the info as quickly as you can."

William eased the car out of the parking lot. "What are you going to do?"

"I have to call Lucy." As Eli dialed Lucy's cellphone number, an overwhelming concern for her safety invaded his thoughts.

The noise in the high school gym was oppressive. Fans stomped their feet and the wheelchair rugby players rolled out onto the court. Lucy sat between Nelson and Heather. Dawson waved as he glided by on the court. What a ham. Her little brother's smile could brighten an overcast sky.

Heather wrapped her arms through Lucy's. "Your brother is doing so well."

"I was just thinking that myself." Something Eli had said to her floated back into her head. Fear did rule her decisions. She couldn't live in fear of something else bad happening to Dawson or think that she could keep him safe by playing the mother role. When Dawson had had his accident, she'd broken an engagement and put her life on hold. Dawson had recovered fine; she was out of excuses.

She sighed. As upset as she was with him, she had to admit, Eli had been right about a lot of things. She pulled out her cell phone and stared at the photo of her and Eli. She should just delete the picture. He had been deceptive in a big way, too. Why couldn't she let him go?

Nelson passed Lucy some nachos and leaned in to see what she was looking at. "That guy, huh?"

"What, you don't like him?"

"He seems all right, I guess."

Nelson shrugged. On the court, the referee blew the whistle and tossed the ball in the air.

She brushed her finger over the photograph. "I don't know what to think about him."

Nelson took a bite of corn chip and wrapped an arm around Lucy. "I think you should just hang out with your friends and forget about him."

Heather leaned against Lucy. She had to speak directly into Lucy's ear to be heard above the thunder of the game and roar of the crowd. "I disagree. I think you should give him a chance to explain."

"You guys are like having the good angel on one shoulder and the bad angel on the other." She flipped her phone shut. "I just can't figure out who is who."

Though she couldn't hear the ring, her phone vibrated in her hand. She checked the number; Eli was calling her. Her arm muscles tensed as it rang two and then three times. All the anger and hurt she had felt earlier returned. She couldn't talk to him now. The wound was still too new. She clicked off her phone and snapped it shut again.

Best to focus on the game. Dawson stole the ball from an opponent and passed it to a team member. Lucy jumped up and cheered along with the rest of the crowd, but her heart wasn't in it. Thoughts of Eli danced around the edges of her mind. Memories of the warmth of his voice and the way his kiss made her head spin rose to the surface. Why couldn't he just have told her about the investigation? At least now she understood why he had been so protective of her. Had his need to keep her safe turned into something more or had it all been lies? She gritted her teeth. For sure, she wouldn't have let herself fall for him if she'd known he wasn't going to be around long.

An opponent crashed into Dawson's wheelchair, causing one wheel to catch air. Lucy gasped. Heather squeezed her shoulder. "He's all right. You can't control what happens on the court by being afraid and worrying about him from your seat."

Lucy smiled. So many of her reactions were because of fear. Maybe she was afraid of loving Eli because that would mean she risked losing someone again. Lucy sat up a little straighter. She had used the news about the investigation as an excuse to pull away from him. "Thanks, Heather, you gave me my answer. You are the good angel."

She stood up and edged past Nelson in his seat.

Nelson drew his legs up. "Where are you going?" He grimaced.

She leaned over to shout into Nelson's ear to be heard above the noise of the game. "I have to make an important phone call."

Lucy took the steps up through the bleachers two at a time. The area around the concession stands was a little quieter. She had instantly assumed that if they lived in different cities, the relationship would be impossible. There were rivers in Spokane, too. Maybe she could move to

Spokane. Maybe they could make this work long distance. It didn't matter. They would figure it out together.

A small cluster of people swarmed over to the concession window. Lucy walked through the hallways of the school, trying to find a quieter spot. She turned down a corridor.

Most of the high school classrooms were filled with kids. When she peeked inside one of them, it was obvious that a speech and debate competition was going on.

She leaned against the wall and stared at her phone. Her hair fell in front of her face as her finger hovered over the buttons. Sometimes you just had to do things even if you were afraid.

"Lucy Kimbol, it's been a long time."

Lucy looked up. "Coach Whitmore." His big-toothed smile oozed false charm. "What are you doing here?"

"I'm doing some volunteer coaching." He reached up and touched her hair. She jerked back. He leaned toward her. "I'd recognize that dark mane anywhere." One side of his lips curled. "You still playing ball?"

Lucy took two steps back and planted her feet. Even though her heart raced and her legs were shaking, she injected strength into her voice. "I have outgrown playing basketball." And she had outgrown being intimidated by him. "If you'll excuse me, I have things to do."

She whirled around and strode down the slanted ramp. Even though she didn't glance back, she could sense him staring at her.

She turned down another hallway, releasing a heavy breath as she braced her hand against the wall. How easy it was to feel like a defenseless teenager again. Lucy lifted her chin and pushed off the wall. She wasn't defenseless, and she wasn't alone in this world. So much had changed since high school.

She glanced down two diverging hallways. When she had gone to school here, the kids had called this section of the building the labyrinth. Most of it was underground, with no windows and widely spaced lights on the ceiling, half of which were burned out.

One way led to the band room. Judging from the number of people coming up that hallway, the band room was probably being used for speech presentations. The noise up the hallway increased, and kids spilled out of the classrooms. The other hallway would be quieter for talking to Eli.

The end of the hallway led to an open door. Clicking on a light revealed a weight room with wrestling mats. The single light hanging from the center of the ceiling did little to illuminate the dark corners. She had never been in here before, but at least it was quiet.

Lucy sat on a weight bench and dialed Eli's number. The phone rang four times then went to voice mail. Her shoulders slumped. Just when she had worked up the courage to talk to him.

She took in a deep breath to loosen the tension in her rib cage. She stared again at the picture of her and Eli, heads together, the river glistening in the background.

Her phone rang.

"Did you just try to call me?" Eli's voice sounded frantic.

"Yes, Eli, I—"

"Where are you right now? Who are you with?"

"Eli I have something to say to you, and if I don't say it now, I might lose my courage."

"Where are you at?"

Was he even hearing her? "I told you earlier. I'm at Dawson's tournament."

"Who is there with you?"

The room went dark. Lucy tilted her head. "Just a second, the light just burned out."

She stood up to make her way to the door toward the light that spilled in from the hallway.

The door whooshed shut, blocking out all illumination. Lucy's foot caught on the corner of a mat; she stumbled, managing to catch herself before she fell. Her phone flew out of her hand and skittered out in front of her someplace in the darkness.

She dropped down on her knees, sweeping her hand in wide arcs as she felt for her phone. She worked her fingers along the hard, cold vinyl of a mat.

Her shoulder brushed against a piece of exercise equipment, and then her head rammed into another part of the machine. She winced as the pain radiated through her scalp. She sat up, rubbing the sore spot on her forehead.

The silence enveloped her. Her throat went dry. Lucy fought to make out even outlines in the dim room. She blinked. If she just gave it a minute, her eyes would adjust. A thought nagged her just below the surface of awareness, but she refused to give in to it.

Again on her hands and knees, she swept the area around her. No phone. No matter how hard she tried not to think about it, the sequence of events streamed through her head. Her pulse drummed in her ears. It was normal for a lightbulb to suddenly burn out. But as she replayed what had just happened, she knew that doors did not close by themselves in a place where there was no wind.

Lucy felt the object in front of her. The cold metal of a weight bench. With her heart racing, she slipped onto the bench. She tapped her feet on the wooden floor, willing objects to be discernible in the blackness. Was there someone else in the room with her?

This part of the school was far away from the activity that was going on. She stopped tapping her feet. Despite her effort at not allowing the thoughts to fully blossom, memories of being attacked in her own home came back. That assailant had used darkness as a weapon, too.

"Coach Whitmore?" she whispered.

Lucy scanned from right to left. She listened. She squeezed her eyes shut. Her body trembled with fear.

Come on, Lucy, pull it together.

In an effort to slow her racing heart, she took in two deep, slow breaths. There had to be an explanation. Could someone have seen the light on, switched it off and closed the door without noticing that she was in here? That had to be it. Seeing Coach Whitmore had just spooked her.

The tightness between her shoulders let up. She just needed to get to the door, open it and turn on the light. She rose to her feet and moved in the direction where the door and light switch would most likely be.

Even though she swung her hands out in front of her, she ran into pieces of equipment. A metal bar grazed the side of her head. Her foot rammed against a stack of free weights.

She reached out. The door had to be around here somewhere. Her hand touched the bumpy surface of the wall, and she felt along it. She continued to pat the wall. Her finger touched the sleek paper of a poster. She hadn't been in the room long enough to note where things were. The wall came to an end, and she followed along the second wall. There were only four walls. Sooner or later, she would find the door.

The sound of metal tinkling against metal caused every muscle in her body to contract. Her breath caught. Someone was moving through the room and must have bumped against the exercise equipment. Lucy turned in the direction she'd heard the noise. Her heart raced.

Frantic, she felt up and down the wall. She patted quickly across the surface until she found a hinge. She reached across the expanse of metal at the height where the doorknob should be. She breathed in a shallow, quick breath.

Her finger wrapped around the metal of the doorknob. She angled her wrist and turned.

A sound that was almost like rush of wind surrounded her, and then a hard mass bashed into her. Lucy fell, hitting the floor on her back. Shock waves of pain burst out from her spine. She couldn't breathe. The wind had been knocked out of her. She wheezed in air that felt like it was filled with pebbles.

Her body shuddered from the impact as she lay in the darkness.

Even before she could catch her breath, a cold grip like iron wrapped around her wrist. She struggled to break free, clawing at his arm with her free hand. Her attacker grabbed her at the collar and pulled her close. His hot breath stained her face. She angled away so she was on her stomach. He clamped onto her arm and twisted it behind her back, pushing upward.

Her muscles flared from the pain. Why was this man doing this to her?

"Please," she cried.

Her stomach pressed against the hardwood floor. Did he mean to kill her or just torment her?

"Whhyyyyyy?" she sputtered.

A foot jabbed into her back. He grabbed her wrists and slipped something around them. When she wiggled to get away, he smashed his boot harder against her spine.

She moaned in protest as the shock of pain immobilized her.

"What...what...are you going to do?"

Her cheek pressed against the cool floor. She waited for her breathing to even out. Her shoulder and arm muscles strained.

Her assailant finished tying her hands with a final jerk to tighten the knot. The weight lifted off her back. She angled to one side to try to get up. The coolness of metal grazed her neck. He had a gun.

There was no way she could get away from this man.

FOURTEEN

Eli gripped the steering wheel and pressed the accelerator even harder. He tried Lucy's cell one more time. It went straight to message. He didn't know Dawson's number.

Mountain Springs wasn't that big. How many places could they hold a tournament anyway? He slowed as he drove past a workout place that he knew had a basketball court. There were only a few cars in the lot.

Eli hit his blinker and pulled into a parking lot. He had no idea where the high school was in this town, but it seemed like the most likely place for a tournament.

He phoned the police station. He recognized Officer Spitz's gravelly voice. William must have gone somewhere to track down the information he needed. Eli alerted Spitz to the situation and got directions to the high school.

"Who did you say might be in some kind of trouble?" Spitz cleared his throat.

"Lucy Kimbol."

Eli counted four seconds of silence on the other end of the line.

"I am really concerned. We got cut off from a phone conversation. I heard a scream." Eli kept his voice in a monotone to subdue his ire. He had spoken to all the men about this. It didn't matter what the department thought of Lucy. An officer was sworn to keep everyone safe regardless of their feelings about that person.

"I'll send some…some men over," Officer Spitz stuttered.

Eli stared at the ceiling of his car. Could the guy sound any more reluctant? "This is your chance to prove to Lucy that help comes when it is needed, and that you learned something from the incident four years ago." He turned the key in the ignition.

"You don't know the whole history of this thing."

"History doesn't matter." Eli fought to keep his voice level.

"I said we'll get some men out there."

Eli hung up the phone. He pressed the accelerator and pulled out onto the street.

Please, God, let her be all right.

He steadied his own breathing. The five-block

drive to the high school felt like a million miles. He parked his car and jumped out. The first door he tried was locked. He circled the building to the side that faced a football field and tried another door. He stepped into a long hallway.

The boom of a cheering crowd filtering down the hallway told him he was in the right place. He stepped into the gym. He scanned the crowd, not honing in on anyone who looked familiar.

The wheelchairs sailed down the court. Eli picked out Dawson in a red jersey just as the ball was passed to him. He walked to one side of the bleachers and searched the crowd on the opposite side. He held only a glimmer of hope that his panic had been unfounded and that he would see Lucy's beautiful face at any moment.

Someone tapped him on the shoulder.

He swung around to face a teenage girl with fat red cheeks and round glasses. "You're Lucy's renter. I'm one of her students, Marnie. I come out to her house for lessons."

"Yes, do you know where she is?"

The girl angled her head around Eli so she would have a clearer view of the court and stands. "I saw her in the hallway earlier. I was waiting for my turn to do my speech, and she walked by. I don't think she noticed me, though."

His heart skipped a beat. "Where at? Which way?"

"I can show you." The girl pivoted and headed toward the door. She led him down a series of hallways and then stopped in front of a closed door. "I was in this room. The door was open. We hadn't started yet."

"You saw her pass by?"

"She had her phone in her hand. She looked really happy about something, like glowing." Marnie sighed. "Miss Kimbol is nice, but she always seems like a person who worries about things. It was cool to see her so happy."

"Which way was she going?"

Marnie pointed. "That hallway branches off and you either end up in the band room or the wrestling room."

Eli raced down the ramp. A check of the band room revealed lots of teenagers, but no Lucy and no one who had seen her. He jogged back up the hallway to where it split off, and headed down the second hallway.

He turned the knob on the door, leaned in and flicked on a light. Exercise equipment, discarded T-shirts and wrestling mats filled his field of view.

The room was empty.

* * *

Lucy sat in the darkness with the smell of her own perfume heavy in the air. She'd been tied up and blindfolded with the scarves that had been stolen from her place; the aroma of her perfume was still evident on them. Her wrists hurt from being bound so tightly. How much time had passed since he had brought her here? An hour maybe. Her kidnapper moved around the room. She picked out some distinct noises: the sear of something hitting a hot frying pan, a faucet running, feet stomping on wood.

He'd dragged her out a back door of the school and across a nearly empty parking lot. He hadn't blindfolded her until he'd thrown her in the back of the car and told her to be quiet.

Even though she hadn't been able to see, she had tried to pay attention to when the car had turned and what noises she'd heard. They had driven maybe twenty minutes. When he'd pulled her from the car, the scent of pine was heavy in the air and the ground was mushy beneath her feet. She was probably in a cabin not far from Mountain Springs. What were the chances of anyone finding her? There must be a dozen cabins that close to town. Lucy curled her bound hands into fists, refusing to give in to despair. There had to be a way to escape.

She bent her elbows in an effort to loosen her bindings, which only made her shoulders hurt. With her fingers, she scraped the area around her and felt fabric, probably a quilt. She had heard the creak of springs when he had tossed her here.

Judging from the loudness of the noises, the cabin must have had an open layout. The salty scent of ham cooking filled the air, and she heard more footsteps. Things were being mixed and stirred. Even before he had spoken, she had known who her kidnapper was. All the pieces had fallen into place. He had been the one stalking her in high school, and he had started again when he'd returned to Mountain Springs.

"Are you hungry?" A cupboard door slammed.

A chill crept over her body when he spoke. "I could use some water." Her words were strained.

She heard running water, and a moment later, he stomped across the floor. His touch on her neck made her recoil. The rim of a glass pressed against her lips and she drank. Her throat felt like it had been clawed by a cat.

He pulled the glass away.

"Why are you doing this?"

"Because I love you. I've always loved you."

His voice made her skin crawl. "I wish I could at least see."

"All right, my love." His rough fingers grazed her temples as he slipped the scarf off the top of her head. "Better?"

She nodded and looked into the face of her stalker, Nelson Thane. He had hidden his obsession beneath a veneer of friendliness and concern. As a high school student, she had sensed on some instinctual level that she didn't want to continue a romantic relationship with him, and now she knew why. All this time she had assumed Coach Whitmore, who was so blatant in his advances, had been harassing her in high school. The coach was probably more posturing than action. Instead her stalker had been quiet and polite, a perfect gentleman.

Nelson's lips curled. He glanced around the cabin. "You like it."

All the windows had thick curtains on them. The cabin was sparse in furnishings but she recognized her things, taken from her house, spread out on a dresser: her book, her jewelry and her fly rod. She craned her neck, trying to see what else he had taken. She recognized a picture frame that she thought she had just misplaced. He must have been in her place more times than when she had caught him. All the items were arranged in a tidy pattern. In the kitchen, the distance between the chairs at the table looked like it had been measured to make sure they were spaced at equal distance. She'd be hard-pressed to find a crumb or speck of dust on the floor.

He planted a chair about four feet from her, grabbed a plateful of food from the kitchen counter and sat down to face her. "Are you sure you're not hungry?"

She shook her head.

"You know what I love most about you, Lucy?" He took a bite of ham, making smacking sounds as he chewed. "Your face, so beautiful. And your purity, so untouched, so clean." He reached out and brushed a hand over her cheek. "That is the way you should stay." His teeth showed when he spoke.

Lucy jerked away from his touch as her heartbeat quickened.

He stabbed another piece of ham with his fork. "Sometimes my desire for you was so strong, I had to find…a substitute."

Her throat constricted. What was he talking about? Her memory flashed on the photographs that had been spread out on Eli's desk.

She could not form the words in her head. Nelson continued to chew, careful to dab his mouth with a napkin after almost every bite. She let out a moan that was almost a scream. Who was this monster in front of her?

Nelson chattered, oblivious to her increasing terror. "I was okay with being your friend. The online dating thing only bothered me a little. I could tell you didn't like those guys." His voice dropped half an octave. "But then he came along, and I saw the two of you at the river."

Lucy couldn't get a deep breath. Nelson's jealousy of Eli had led to the attack in her place. "Eli is a good detective. He'll find me."

Nelson grinned. "I'm counting on that. He's a smart man, and I think I left enough clues. My landlady has a big mouth. The gun I brought isn't for you." Nelson stopped eating and studied Lucy, his eyes cutting through her. "It's for him."

Lucy's stomach roiled. She tasted bile and her eyes watered. "Why?"

He jumped to his feet, threw his plate against the wall and shouted, "Because you are supposed to love me!"

She leaned away from him as the shattering of glass echoed in her ear.

Nelson crumpled at her feet, gripping her legs and peering up at her. "Why can't you look at me like you looked at him?"

His fingers dug into her knees, and she steeled herself, trying not to pull back and reveal her repulsion.

"Nelson, this isn't right—you have to stop." How long did she have before Eli found the cabin and ran straight into his death?

He reached up and ran the back of his hand over her cheek. She pressed her feet harder into the floor and closed her eyes.

Stop touching me.

"Please, Nelson," she whispered. "Don't do this to him."

He rose to his feet and sauntered over to the window, pulling back the dark curtain. "I'm sure he'll be here any minute."

Lucy took in a shallow, sharp breath. It felt like a weight was on her chest. She had to do something. Her feet were still free. She could run, try to knock Nelson over and escape to warn Eli.

Nelson strutted back to the counter, where his hands brushed over the gun, a reminder to her of who held all the power. He glanced in her direction. His eyes became narrow slits.

He stepped away from the counter, leaving the gun. She leaned forward to get more comfortable. He sprang across the room.

He made a *tsk*ing sound and shook his head. "Lucy, always planning and scheming. You think I don't know what you were trying to do." He waggled his finger.

Maybe running right now wasn't such a good idea. Still, she could watch and wait. Sooner or later, he would have a moment of inattention when she could knock him over and get to the door. He might turn his back or even leave the room. All she needed was a few seconds.

"I'm thinking it would be better if you remained in the dark." He lifted the blindfold off the bedpost.

"No, please." How could she hope to help Eli if she couldn't see?

Lucy shook her head and angled away as Nelson tried to slip the scarf back over her eyes. She turned sideways on the bed. He clamped her forearm and yanked her up. His fingers found her neck and suctioned around it. His face was inches from hers.

"Don't. You. Dare." His fingers pressed hard against her throat. She flinched as his spit splattered on her cheeks.

She gurgled. Even as she fought for air, she narrowed her eyes at him. Whatever it took, she would keep Eli alive.

He increased the pressure on her neck. "Don't be so defiant. You are not as strong as you think you are."

He let go of her neck. She gasped. He slipped the blindfold over her eyes. Darkness augmented the thrumming of her heartbeat in her ears. She scooted away from him. She rocked back and forth, praying for strength, praying she would not give up hope, praying for a miracle.

The hours ticked by. Lucy could hear Nelson walking around, turning the pages of a book, opening and closing the refrigerator.

Fog filled her brain, and she nodded off. She lay on the bed and pulled her feet up, sleeping fitfully. When she awoke, she heard the sound of a radio as he flipped through stations, maybe searching for some news about the kidnapping. Radio voices surrounded by static faded in and out.

She wiggled on the bed causing the springs to squeak. Her shoulders ached from having her hands pulled back behind her. The heaviness of sleep crept into her limbs, and she drowsed off again. Images of Eli being shot invaded her dreams.

When she turned slightly on the bed to get more comfortable, she felt something warm on her arm. A moment later, she realized her arm was bleeding. Pushing with her feet, she wiggled around on the bed until she felt something hard; a piece of the broken plate Nelson had thrown against the wall. If it was sharp enough to cut skin, it might be sharp enough to cut through the scarf.

She repositioned herself and angled the piece of porcelain until she felt the tension of it pressing against her bindings.

Nelson paced the floor. At one point, she thought she heard a door open. She sliced at the fabric, not even sure if she was making progress. The bindings seemed to be getting looser. The shard dug into her fingers, and she shuddered as fresh blood oozed from a cut.

She heard the steady creak of a rocking chair for what seemed like hours and then it slowed. Nelson's heavy breathing told her he had fallen asleep.

Lucy pulled at her wrists and moved them up and down. The restraints still felt tight; her shoulder muscles burned. She continued to tear through the fabric.

Sometime in the night, Nelson rose from the chair, walked across the floor and touched her hair. She lay on her side, so her wrists were not visible. Nelson kissed her forehead.

Lucy held her breath and waited for the sounds of his fading footsteps. He hovered over her. His clothes rustled.

Just go away. Get away from me.

Finally, he walked away, and she heard the creak of the rocking chair again. She sawed the jagged porcelain across the fabric. The listlessness of sleep permeated her mind and then her muscles. Her cutting slowed and she drowsed.

Eli parked the SUV he was driving on the side of the mountain road. He spoke into the two-way radio. "We stop here and hike in the rest of the way. We don't want to risk him hearing us coming."

William clicked on his night-vision goggles and pushed open the passenger-side door. A female officer got out of the backseat.

It had taken precious time to get the warrant to search Nelson Thane's place, to locate the cabin and to track Jessica's movements the day she died. On her last day alive, Jessica had delivered sandwiches to a teacher's workshop in Cragmore that Nelson had been attending.

Eli put on his night-vision goggles, too. Staging this in the dark had its advantages. Nelson would be tired by now, maybe even sleeping. There was less chance of detection.

A second vehicle pulled up. Officers O'Bannon, Spitz and Peterson got out.

Officers Spitz and O'Bannon had been cooperative. Another officer named Clark had been pulled from a town ten miles from Mountain Springs. Peterson had insisted on being part of the team. "To make things right," he had said.

"When we get within a hundred yards of the house, get off the road. O'Bannon and Spitz to the back of the house. Peterson and Clark cover the sides. Springer and I will go in by the front. I don't know how many exit points we are dealing with. He may try to run." He swallowed to clear the lump in his throat. "He may try to harm Lucy."

William slapped Eli's back. "We'll get her out."

Eli squared his shoulders. "Yeah, we will." His heart hammered at a frantic rate. He pushed from consciousness images of harm coming to Lucy and focused on the road in front of him. Whatever it took, he was not going to lose Lucy.

His hand brushed over his pistol in its holster. Up ahead, the murky glow of a barely discernible light caused the men and woman to slip into the darkness of the forest.

Lucy jerked awake. How much time had passed? Ten minutes or five hours? She had no way of knowing. Nelson wasn't making any noise. The drip-drip-drip of water hitting the stainless steel sink pressed on her ears.

The skin on her fingers stung from where she had cut it. Where was Eli? Despair threatened to overtake her. What were Nelson's plans for her?

He had spared her once, but he had killed all those other women.

Lucy shivered as she propped herself up to a sitting position. "Nelson?"

No reply.

She jerked forward and rose to her feet, wobbling slightly. She swept her feet in half circles in front of her to detect where the furniture was. A door creaked open. Footsteps echoed across the floor.

The scent of cologne and hair gel surrounded her. "Trying to escape again, huh?"

All the air left her lungs.

Nelson was breathing heavily as though he had run a great distance.

He pulled the blindfold off, digging his fingernails into her forehead. "I've been watching the forest. They're on their way. I'm sure he'll be the first one through the door. Do you want to watch him die?"

Blood trickled past her temple. He pushed her into the kitchen, yanked open a drawer and pulled out some duct tape. She pressed the heels of her hands together hoping he wouldn't notice that the fabric was frayed where she had been cutting it.

He put the gun in a holster around his waist. Sweat glistened on his forehead as he forced her back to the bed, pushed her down and placed a knee on her stomach.

When she angled to get away, he increased the pressure on her chest. He tore off a length of duct tape and used his teeth to make a small tear in it.

He smashed the duct tape against her mouth. "You'll be able to watch, but you won't be able to warn."

Grabbing her by the collar, he pulled her to a sitting position. Lucy's heart pounded as tears and blood trailed down her face.

Nelson cranked open a window. "I'll be able to hear them coming," he explained. He kicked the door shut with his foot and pulled the gun from its holster. He positioned himself behind the door so that when it was flung open he would have a clear shot at the man's back—Eli's back. "I know that Mr. Hero will be the first one in. I just know it."

While she worked her wrists up and down to break free of the tightly tied scarves, she memorized the layout of the cabin. The door that led to the road and one window lined the south-facing wall. On the other side was a door that probably led to the bathroom. There might be a small window in there, but the kitchen had no windows or back door.

Nelson adjusted his hand on the gun and pressed his back against the wall.

The silence was oppressive. Eli must be moving

in on foot. Who had come with him? Could she even hope that the Mountain Springs Police Department would help when they found out she was the kidnap victim?

Lucy's breathing became labored. She fought to keep her shoulders still while she worked her hands loose. If she could free herself in time, she could get the duct tape off and scream a warning to Eli. She had no way of knowing if Nelson would shoot her or not. It was a chance she had to take. She'd do anything to save Eli. With her fingers she felt a weakness in the fabric. As she increased the size of the tear, the bindings loosened.

Nelson pushed away from the wall. He had taken off his shoes at the door, his stocking feet barely making noise as he tiptoed to the window. Using the barrel of the gun, he pulled the curtain back and peered outside.

Lucy leaned forward to see out the window. She caught only a flash of darkness.

"What do you suppose is taking him so long?" A subtext of panic girded his words.

Her throat was raw from crying, and the duct tape made it hard to breathe.

Nelson whirled around and glared at her with the coldest eyes she had ever seen. She froze, fearing that he would notice that she had been working at getting her hands free. Sweat stung her eyes as her heart pounded with an insane intensity. She steeled her gaze and looked right at him. She was not about to let him see her fear.

Nelson turned. This time when he looked out the window, his shoulder spasmed. She detected a twitch in his cheek when he glanced at her. He'd seen something. He took long strides across the floor and slammed his back against the wall behind the door. He adjusted the grip on the gun as he raised it.

Lucy's leg muscles tensed. She leaned forward, not daring to take in a breath. Nelson's gaze darted to the window and then back to Lucy.

The door burst open. A man ran in. The blast of a gun enveloped Lucy. Glass shattered.

FIFTEEN

Eli kicked open the door and pressed his back against the south-facing wall. His heart lurched when he saw Lucy bound and gagged on the bed.

In the same instant that Nelson stepped from behind the door, William burst through the window. Nelson averted his gaze toward William, causing the gun to jerk up. The glass lamp beside Eli shattered into a thousand pieces.

Eli lunged toward Nelson, circling his waist and knocking him to the floor. The gun fell out of Nelson's hand and skittered across the floor. The footsteps of the other officers coming in thundered on the floorboards. William scrambled to his feet to help subdue Nelson.

Eli raced across the room to Lucy.

He cupped her face in his hands. "Are you all right? Did he hurt you?"

Her face was bloody and tearstained. She pulled her hands from behind her back and tossed a shredded scarf to the floor. She wrapped her arms around him.

Eli's throat tightened from the strength of the emotions he felt. He buried his face in her hair, drowning in her sweet honey scent. "I'll do whatever it takes to stay here with you. I meant it when I said I wouldn't leave you."

She pulled back and gazed at him with those blue eyes. She reached up to peel the duct tape off her mouth.

He brushed her hand away. "Let me." Slowly, gently he removed the tape.

"Nelson was going to kill you." She touched shaking fingers to her lips.

"But he didn't." He went to grab her hand and then noticed the cuts. The rage over what Nelson had done returned. "I thought you said he didn't hurt you."

"I did that. To cut myself loose."

"Wait here." Eli rummaged through cupboards, looking for a first-aid kit.

The other men took a handcuffed Nelson out of the cabin.

Eli returned to Lucy and sat on the bed beside her. "Give me your hand."

Her skin felt like silk against his calloused hand. She leaned toward him as he placed a Band-Aid on the cut. The look of warmth and affection on her face drew him in.

Lucy shook her head. "All these years, I thought it was somebody else. I have to tell the coach I'm sorry. I need to apologize to O'Bannon and Spitz, too, for pointing the finger at their friend."

"You were just a scared kid looking for help." Eli held her hand, brushing his thumb over each of her knuckles.

"Still, I need to own my part in what caused this mess. It should go a long way toward mending things between us." Lucy leaned closer to Eli. "Why didn't I see what Nelson was doing?"

"Nobody could have seen it. He hid it well. The key was the calendar in Jessica's house. All the women died on school holidays. We found Nelson's laptop. He was signed up with the dating service under a different name. He lied about where he lived so he fell outside the parameters of the profile. Nelson killed Jessica on impulse because she looked so much like you."

Lucy shuddered and instinctually Eli tightened his embrace.

"Something Greg said made me realize the robberies were connected to the killing. When we showed him the pictures of the other women he said, 'They all look like Lucy, only not as pretty.'

Nelson's obsession with you was the reason for his crimes. You weren't just one more potential victim. You were the whole focus of the crimes."

Lucy gasped and her hand fluttered to her neck. "Those poor women."

"You're safe now," Eli said. "Something must have triggered the escalation to him kidnapping you."

"I fell in love, and he saw it when I was at Dawson's game. That's why he attacked me in my place after we went fishing. That's why he wanted…he wanted to hurt you." Her fingers touched his lips.

"You fell in love?" he asked.

"Yes." She tilted her head, put her hand on the back of his neck and pulled him toward her. "With you," she said as their lips met.

EPILOGUE

The drive out to the river where Eli knew he would find Lucy went by in a flash. Several of her students lined up on the rocky beach. The trees had just begun to turn gold and red. Lucy pushed a boat away from the shore. She stepped into the boat and lifted the oar. She set the oar down when she saw Eli coming toward her.

Four months had passed since Nelson had been arrested. Eli had testified at his trial less than a week ago and Thane soon would be sentenced and locked away. It was over. Lucy was safe. The investigation no longer stood between him and the woman he loved. Today, the things Nelson had taken out of Lucy's place had been released from the evidence room.

Eli splashed through the river, oblivious to the autumn chill of the water. He grabbed the boat.

Lucy laughed. "What is all this about? Did the

chief say they would hire you so you can be a small-town cop?"

In the months they had waited for the trial, Eli had been back and forth to Spokane. Even though she was open to the idea, he couldn't take Lucy away from this river and people who loved her. Eli shook his head. "I got a better idea." He pulled the boat toward him, savoring the delight he felt at being close to her.

She placed a warm palm on his cheek. "So you didn't get the job, but you are still excited."

"I don't know why I didn't think of it sooner."

A mystified expression crossed her beautiful features. "What are you talking about?"

"You said that originally this business was supposed to be run by you and your brother."

"It would be a lot easier, sure. With extra help, I could grow the business. Dawson was supposed to be my partner, but…"

"Not Dawson. Me."

"But you're a cop. It's what you do."

"I have not only fallen in love with you, I've fallen in love with this river." His heart raced in anticipation of what he was about to say. "Lucy?"

A sudden breath escaped her lips. "Yes." She sat up straighter.

He pulled a small envelope out of his pocket.

The envelope he had gotten out of the evidence room this morning. "I want to be your business partner." He opened the bag and pulled out Lucy's grandmother's ring. "And I would love it if we could do it as man and wife."

Lucy gazed at him; her blue eyes sparkled. "Oh, Eli."

He slid the ring on her finger. "I thought we could get married here at the river. The place where I first knew I loved you."

Lucy's eyes grew wide and round. She nodded then lunged toward Eli, wrapping her arms around him. She knocked him backward. They fell into the knee-deep water, laughing. The sun hinged on the towering mountains above them. The river, glistening like silver, rippled and swirled around them.

* * * * *

Dear Reader,

Like Lucy, I have had the privilege of growing up surrounded by God's natural beauty for all my life. As a child, my parents planned weekend picnics to the river. My sisters and I waded through clear rocky streams and mushy-bottomed ponds, catching frogs while my dad panned for gold.

A forest surrounded the trailer court where we lived when I was in elementary school. I found a special flat rock in an aspen grove where I would go to sit and think for hours. Later when we moved out to the country, the juniper forest provided a place for my imagination to flourish as I played made-up games with my sisters. The hills that surrounded our property gave us ample opportunity to go sledding in the winter and take daredevil bike rides in the summer.

Even now as a busy mom, I seek the solace that nature provides. A hiking trail is only yards from our front door; I often use my walks for a time to pray and get clarity on the problems I face. The mountains and the rivers are within minutes of my home. All of it is a beautiful reminder of what a creative artist God is. The verse in Romans 1:20 says that God's "eternal power and divine nature—have been clearly seen, being understood from what he has made." We understand God better when we connect with nature.

It may be that your contact with nature is the trees in a nearby park or the flowers that bloom in your windowsill garden. Whatever it is, I encourage you to be nourished and renewed by the natural beauty that surrounds us all. Nature in all its forms is a gift from God, showing us how much He loves us.

Sharon J. Turner

QUESTIONS FOR DISCUSSION

1. Because she had to depend on herself at an early age, Lucy has a hard time asking for help. Have you ever struggled with asking for help?

2. Lucy is heartbroken when her jewelry is taken, not because it has monetary value but because it connects her to people she has loved and lost. Do you have special treasures that remind you of people who were important to you?

3. Do you think Eli made a good choice to help Lucy get her boat out of the river, even when she resisted? Could his plan have backfired?

4. Lucy says that she loves being on the river because it connects her with God in such a strong way. Outside of church, what ways do you find to connect to God?

5. As a river guide, Lucy's job provides an inconsistent income, but she cannot imagine doing anything else because she loves it so much. Have you ever made financial sacrifices to do

a job you loved? Or have you ever done a job you didn't like because the income was good? What was the result of your choice?

6. Heather's online matchmaking is well intentioned because she wants Lucy to find love and happiness. Have you ever had a friend who did things out of love but really didn't understand your need? How did you handle the situation to preserve the friendship?

7. Like Lucy, all of us have wounds from the past that make it hard for us to trust and to let people get close to us. What steps have you taken to find healing for your wounds?

8. How important do you think a supportive church community is in helping us grow and heal?

9. Because of bad past experience with the police, Lucy no longer believes they will help her. Has an organization or a person ever broken your trust because they let you down when you expected help? Explain.

10. All of us have a different turning point in our faith journey. Lucy became a Christian as a

teenager when she faced the loss of her mother. Eli's turning point happened when he came face-to-face with evil in his police work. What was your turning point?

11. Lucy has suffered a great deal of loss in her life, and it has made her afraid to love. Can you think of a loss in your own life, big or small? How has it affected your outlook and responses?

12. As a police officer, Eli wants to protect potential victims. While this is a noble goal, he ultimately realizes he can't protect everyone all the time. He finds peace when he realizes God is still in control no matter what happens. Has there ever been a time when you thought you could control a situation, only to discover you had no control?

13. In order to do his job, Eli has to keep a secret from Lucy. What was the fallout from that choice? Could he have done something different?

14. One of the police officers takes deliberate steps to restore Lucy's faith in the police. What

does Lucy do to repair her relationship with the police department? How does Eli help?

15. To make their future together work, Eli comes up with an interesting solution. Do you think it was the best choice? What else could he have done?

Here's a sneak preview of
THE RANCHER'S PROMISE
by Jillian Hart
Available in June 2010
from Love Inspired.

"So, are you back to stay?" Justin's deep voice hid any shades of emotion. Was he fishing for information or was he finally about to say "I told you so"?

"I'll probably go back to teaching in Dallas, but things could change. I'll just have to wait and see." The things in life she used to think were so important no longer mattered. Standing on her own two feet, building a life for herself, healing her wounds—that did.

"And this man you married?" he asked. "Did he leave you or did you leave him?"

"He threw me out." She waited for Justin's reaction. Surely a man with that severe a frown on his face was about to take delight in the irony. She'd turned down Justin's love, and her husband of five years had thrown away hers. If she were Justin, she would want her off his land.

"You were nothing but honest with me back

then." He leaned against the railing, the wind raking his dark hair, and a different emotion passed across his hard countenance. "I was the one who never listened. I loved you so much, I don't think I could hear anything but what I wanted."

"I loved you, too. I wish I could have been different for you." Helpless, she took another step toward the driveway. She didn't know how to thank him. He could be treating her a lot worse right now, and she would deserve it. "Goodbye, Justin."

"I suppose you need a job?"

"I'll figure out something." Need a job? No, she was frantic for one. How did she tell him the truth?

Find out in THE RANCHER'S PROMISE.
Available June 2010 from Love Inspired.